THE SOARING HEART

Menna Williams is a talented woman, determined to make her own way in a male-dominated world. When she becomes housekeeper at Bryn Hyfryd, Menna has grander dreams in mind and, with the help of the dashing Tal Lloyd, it seems they will become reality. But Tal's younger brother, Rhodri, is constantly warning Menna about Tal's reckless nature. Gwenan Lloyd, mistress of Bryn Hyfryd, has problems of her own to overcome. Which of her two nephews, Tal or Rhodri, should she trust?

HEATHER PARDOE

◆

THE SOARING HEART

Complete and Unabridged

LINFORD
Leicester

First published in Great Britain in 2005

First Linford Edition
published 2006

British Library CIP Data

Pardoe, Heather
    The soaring heart.—Large print ed.—
Linford romance library
    1. Love stories
    2. Large type books
    I. Title
    823.9'2 [F]

ISBN 1–84617–304–3

Published by
F. A. Thorpe (Publishing)
Anstey, Leicestershire

Set by Words & Graphics Ltd.
Anstey, Leicestershire
Printed and bound in Great Britain by
T. J. International Ltd., Padstow, Cornwall

This book is printed on acid-free paper

1

'So you're sure there will be someone there to meet you?' Rhys Williams drew his gaze away from the fast-approaching harbour to look down anxiously into the delicate heart-shaped face of his niece. On either side of them the paddles of the little steam boat turned steadily, churning the blue-green water of the Irish Sea into sparkling white foam in the light of a chill autumn dawn.

'Yes, of course.' Menna tucked her arm through his, and smiled at him with all the confidence she should be feeling at this moment, but wasn't feeling at all. 'Harri Jacobs. The gardener, Miss Lloyd wrote in her letter. With a pony and trap. And I bet there won't be many of them at Beaumaris Harbour. I expect they're all so posh on the island they all drive automobiles.'

Rhys grunted at the humour in her tone. Anglesey people were a strange lot, in his opinion, not quite like the people of mainland Snowdonia where Rhys had been born and bred, and quite the sort to indulge in such foolish extravagance.

Mind you, he reflected, turning back to where the shores of this alien place were growing larger by the moment, this new craze for automobiles seemed quite unstoppable. Ever since that Telford fellow had put the road bridge over the river beside Conwy Castle, not even the mediaeval walls of Rhys' home town had been able to keep out the ever-increasing numbers of the noisy little machines racing through, even more of a menace, in his eyes at least, to the dogs and children of the town than the more recent railway snaking its way along the outskirts.

'Well if you're sure. I'm waiting to see, mind, and if you don't like the look of him I'm taking you straight back.'

'But Uncle — '

'Now don't you be worrying, *cariad*, we'd manage somehow. That Miss Lloyd is said to be, well, a bit of a strange one, you know.' Comes of being an old maid, he added to himself. Not that he'd say such a thing to his niece, who at twenty-three was well on the road to being an old maid herself, despite being a pretty little thing with those large eyes, the deep blue of the sea in summer, and the thick mass of dark hair already escaping from the demure bun at the back of her head.

And then there had been the incident of turning down that very respectable offer, and getting quite hysterical about it when, being the responsible uncle he was, he'd pointed out the advantages of the match. Rhys frowned at the memory. All things considered, he was not at all sure this post with the stubbornly independent Miss Lloyd was the best thing for his niece. He cleared his throat, awkwardly. 'I promised your dad I'd look after you.'

'I know. And you have done. You've

done more than I ever could have expected, letting me live with you this summer and finding me the work at the Castle Hotel, but you can't carry on with that over the winter, now the tourists have gone. I have to earn my living somehow.'

Menna knew as well as he did that during the winter months Rhys earned far less from ferrying visitors up the Conwy Valley in his little steam boat to take the waters at the ancient Roman spa at Trefriw, just where the foothills of Snowdon began. For much of the time he would be out with the mussel fishermen from Conwy quay, trying to make what he could to keep his little family in food and rent until the spring. A new mouth to feed was the last thing they needed.

'You could always go back to the studio. I'm sure Sam Makepeace would be glad.'

'No.' Menna turned her head away into the salt spray being blown from the paddles, her voice sharp. She could never go back to the photographic studio. Never. She'd scrub floors, or gut fish on Conwy quay, first, or go out herself with the mussel fishermen throughout the freezing months of winter.

Anything rather than have to step through those doors and meet the knowing smirk of Guto, Sam Makepeace's weasel-faced son. But how could she ever explain this to Uncle Rhys? If he ever knew of what Sam Makepeace had done, and, even more, what Guto had tried to do, she was certain her uncle would not rest until he had the two of them lying at the bottom of the Conwy.

'But Menna, that is what your dad wanted you to do. It was always his dream that you'd take over his side of the partnership.' He patted the small box clutched firmly to her with a smile. 'That's why he trained you up there, Menna. That's why he bought you that camera, so you could have one of your very own. He always said you were the

5

best photographer there. I still have people asking for you to take their portraits. You can't give it up now, cariad. You're like your dad, it's in your blood.'

'I know. And I will go back to it one day. I can't bear it for now. It reminds me too much — ' Menna winced at the lie, and the sympathy and understanding on her uncle's face. It had been painful at first, just after Dad died, being amongst his things, working where she had always been able to look up and meet his smile, or see him charming a bored child in the little studio, or concentrating hard in the dark-room at the back of the building, making sure a print turned out just right.

But after a few months she had found it a comfort just being there, taking over the tasks he used to do. She felt that he was with her, guiding every move.

Until, that is, Sam Makepeace had made it quite plain how he felt about having a woman as a business partner, and Guto had made his intentions even plainer. And they might have sweet-talked Uncle Rhys and Aunt Margaret into believing a marriage with Guto was the most sensible option, but the night Guto had caught her working late, and alone in the studio had left Menna with no doubts as to what kind of marriage it would be.

Menna shivered, clutching the camera box even closer, her fingers tracing the almost-invisible stain along the sharp edges of one side of the box. However much she had scrubbed, she'd never quite been able to remove the last bit of Guto's blood where she'd brought the edges of the box into sharp contact with his nose, and dampened his ardour just long enough for her to escape.

That night she'd been glad she'd had to give up the rent on the house she and Dad had shared next door to the studio and live with Uncle Rhys and his family.

She'd never gone back. Uncle Rhys had found her the work in the hotel for the summer, hoping, she knew, that she would come to her senses and change her mind.

'Well, we're nearly there.' Rhys straightened as the paddle boat made its dignified way between the moored boats of fishermen towards the quay where the boats owners were watching with open curiosity the novel sight of a paddle steamer making its way towards them. 'Still time to turn around, mind.'

'No, thank you,' Menna returned, with a smile softening the determination in her tone. Rhys sighed in defeat, and turned to concentrate on the task of sailing the little boat up to the quay without any mishap.

'I will succeed at this,' Menna told herself. 'I'll be the best housekeeper Miss Lloyd has ever known, I'll be so good she'll never want to let me go.' But go she would. Menna was quite certain of that.

Next summer, when she had saved enough from her wages to put her secret plan into action. It was not just the safety of having a stretch of water, and miles of travel to the nearest bridge between her and Guto Makepeace that had attracted Menna to the post of housekeeper at Bryn Hyfryd. Miss Lloyd's eccentricities did not, it seemed to extend to a lack of generosity towards her staff.

The post of housekeeper was sufficiently well paid to give Menna a hope of being able to save enough to fit out another photographic studio. And this time it would be her studio. Hers. No partners to tell her a woman couldn't possibly be skilled in such a business, let alone succeed. This would be her studio, using all the skills Dad had taught her.

Let Sam Makepeace take away the *Williams and Makepeace* from over the studio door and replace it with his own name alone if he dared. Sam Makepeace, Dad had always said, was a good technician. He could take routine portraits and views of the castle for tourists and print them to perfection.

But he didn't have the eye for light and shade, for balance and dramatic lines, the makings of the kind of photograph that drew the viewer's eyes and would not let them go. The kind of photographs Dad could take.

'And the kind I can take, too,' Menna murmured to herself.

Let Sam and Guto believe they had got rid of her, frightened her away, and made her give up without a fight. They didn't know Menna. Stuck in the studio with Sam giving her the most menial jobs, and with Guto's hands wandering as far as they could go, Menna knew she did not stand a chance. Between them they would have broken her in the end. But with money to start up on her own. A look of determination took over the young woman's face.

Even if she had to start somewhere else, she'd return to the town of her birth one day, she knew it, and with a photographic studio with a reputation that would give Sam Makepeace and his ambitions a run for his money.

As she took her uncle's hand, and stepped out onto the quay, Menna knew there would be no going back. This was the beginning of the most important battle of her life, and no one was about to stop her.

2

'Harri Jacobs. The gardener from Bryn Hyfryd,' Menna explained yet again. Once more the group of fishermen unloading the night's catch on Beaumaris Harbour shook their heads.

'Not seen him in town for weeks, Miss,' volunteered one.

'Wasn't it him whose sister was taken poorly?' said another. 'Married a fisherman from Holyhead,' he added, with mild disapproval of any local girl moving to the far end of the island.

'Could be. Works for Miss Lloyd, does he, *cariad*?'

'Yes, that's the one,' Menna replied eagerly. She was greeted by a general shaking of heads.

'Ah well, that's him, then. You won't be finding him here, *cariad*. His sister's husband was drowned, night before last, in the big storm. Last I heard

Harri had gone up to look after her and the little ones until they're back on their feet, so to speak. Terrible thing,' he added, feelingly.

Menna looked around in despair. She felt very sorry for Harri and his sister, but at the same time it was pressing in on her notice that here was no sign of anything else that looked like any kind of transport suitable for land.

'I'll walk,' she said, at last. 'It can't be that far.'

'Bryn Hyfryd? You'll never find it. Halfway up the coast it is, right round past Penmon Point. You might as well be walking to Holyhead itself. You'd best go back to the mainland, Bryn Hyfryd is no place for a young woman.'

'Especially for a young woman,' one of the older men muttered only just under his breath, causing Rhys Williams to turn from his own questioning with a deep frown. It seemed, Menna realised, that this chance of starting up her own photographic studio was doomed from the start.

Where else was she to find a job that would pay so well without moving way along the cost to the busy centres of Bangor or Caernarfon? She looked round again at the town stretched out in front of her which had seemed so pretty when they'd first arrived with its rows of brightly-painted houses, and the low, perfectly rounded towers of the ancient castle just visible behind.

She was just about to begin questioning the men about the possibility of hiring some kind of transport, or even simply a guide, when the roar of an engine shattered the peaceful dawn of the quayside.

A large black automobile drew up beside them, only just in time, it seemed, to prevent itself from hurtling over the edge of the quay into the water, with a squeal of brakes that sent the seagulls waiting patiently for any scraps that might fall from the catch into a squawking, shrieking cloud encircling their heads.

'Miss Williams?' Through the open

window nearest her, Menna found herself looking into a pair of the darkest brown eyes she had ever seen. Large, luminous eyes, she found herself noting, with flecks of brilliant green around the centre of the iris.

Their owner, she discovered to her annoyance, appeared to find her scrutiny amusing. 'I take it you are Miss Williams,' he added, drily. 'My aunt said you had sharp eyes when she interviewed you. I'm glad to see she wasn't mistaken.'

'I didn't mean to — ' Menna's indignant protest came to an abrupt stop as his words sank in. 'Your aunt?' she demanded. When Miss Lloyd had interviewed her in the hotel in Conwy, along with several other applicants, Menna had heard no mention of any nephew. Particularly not a young, good-looking, automobile-driving nephew. Uncle Rhys would never let her go now!

'That's right. Aunt Gwenan. Miss Lloyd.' His smile became decidedly mischievous. 'I'm sure she'd be mightily flattered you believed her too young to have a nephew of my age.'

'I didn't mean that!' Menna retorted, before she could stop herself. She bit her lip, that was no way to talk to her new employers. To her relief she found he was too busy watching Uncle Rhys making his way towards them to notice her rudeness.

'I see what you do mean,' he remarked softly. With a lithe movement he was out of the automobile in a moment, unfolding into a tall, broad shouldered figure, immaculately dressed in a pale suit, and shaking Uncle Rhys' hand before the older man could even begin to protest. 'You must be Miss Williams' uncle,' he said. 'Pleased to meet you. I'm Rhodri Lloyd, Miss Lloyd's nephew.'

His smile nipped Rhys' scowl neatly in the bud. 'You must forgive this lack of organisation, Mr Williams. I'm afraid Harri Jacobs has been called away on urgent family business, so it was left to me to fill the breach. My fiancée, Lady

Charlotte Wynn, should have accompanied me, but Harri's wife was very upset this morning, and with her being in such a delicate state of health at the moment, if you see what I mean, it was felt unwise to leave her on her own.' His smile broadened, effectively disarming Menna's uncle just as much as the mention of a fiancée from one of the leading families of the area. 'I felt certain you would understand.'

'Of course, Mr Lloyd.' Any doubts in Rhys' mind had clearly vanished. 'It was very good of you to come and fetch Menna.'

'Not at all. Now, if you'll excuse us, my aunt will be getting anxious.'

'Of course.' As Rhodri Lloyd placed Menna's modest bag in the back of the automobile, Rhys kissed his niece affectionately.

'Now you remember, Menna, any doubts and you'll still have a roof over your head.'

'Thank you, Uncle. Give my love to Aunt Margaret, and tell her I'll come and see you all in a few weeks' time.'

As Rhys turned back towards the paddle-steamer, which, by now, was attracting considerable attention from the numerous small boys of the area, Menna found herself being ushered round to the passenger side of the large machine.

'Ever been in one of these before?' Rhodri asked, seeing the slightly nervous expression on her face as he opened the door for her. Menna shook her head. 'Don't worry about it. Safe as houses, these things are. In no time you'll be loving it.'

Inside it smelt of warmth, and new leather, with the faintest hint of engine oil. As she leant back into the rich upholstery of the seat Menna caught the faintest hint of a woman's perfume. It was not the one she remembered Miss Lloyd using at the interview.

Her nephew's fiancée, perhaps. Whoever it belonged to, it lingered with the seductiveness of the more expensive variety. Menna suddenly felt small, horribly aware of the cheap material of her dress, and the worn parts of her shoes no amount of polishing could quite disguise.

Rhodri Lloyd, she suspected, mixed only with the women of the very wealthiest families of the area, who could afford the latest fashions, and never wore their shoes for more than one season.

Wealthy people had frequently come into the photographic studio. Only, somehow, there it had not mattered, not when she was Miss Williams, chosen for her skill in taking sympathetic portraits and busy with her work. Why, all of a sudden it had come to matter at all, was something Menna could not have said.

'Ready, then?' She was distracted by Rhodri Lloyd swinging easily into the seat beside her.

'Yes,' Menna said. She eyed in some alarm the dials and pedals and the huge steering-wheel in front of him. How on earth, she wondered, did anyone ever remember what everything was for? But it was too late for her to do anything about it, for the next moment they were off.

★ ★ ★

'She can reach twenty miles an hour on a straight stretch,' announced Rhodri, proudly.

'Really?' Menna tried to keep her voice below a squeak, and prayed there would be no straight stretches of any kind between Beaumaris and their destination. She could not believe how fast the hedges were flying by, so fast she could barely see them, and how Rhodri had missed the farmer and his cart ambling along in the middle of the road just as they came round a particularly steep bend, Menna would never know.

'Of course, it's nothing when you think of what speeds a train can reach, but designs are improving all the time. I'm certain they'll be able to go twice as fast in no time.

'Really,' she murmured, politely.

'Oh, she's quite safe, you know. If you seriously want to take risks, you should try one of those.'

Menna followed the indication of his head, and discovered a small biplane circling high above them. Menna gasped. She had only seen one such machine before, last year, when a flying machine drifted along the coast and down towards the Menai Straits, although it had been said to crash land in the water long before it got there.

'Is there really someone up there in that?'

'Oh, yes. Ever since Mr Bleriot crossed the Channel in one last summer, they've become quite the rage, you know.' He grinned. 'Me, I'll stick to wheels. It's a long way down if you fall out of that thing.'

'Yes,' Menna agreed, wholeheartedly.

'Of course, Aunt Gwenan is all for them.'

'Really?' Menna tried to imagine the beautifully dressed, rather severe Miss

Lloyd, who had the look of a woman who would disapprove of people enjoying themselves at a village dance on principle, showing any enthusiasm for these new-fangled flying machines.

'Doesn't think they can be a patch on hot-air balloons, of course. She thinks there's no skill in it, you see, the engines do the work for you.' He caught Menna's puzzled expression. 'Hot air balloons take skill, you understand. You have to find the right currents in the air and use them to keep you high, and going in the right direction. Aunt Gwenan is never going to concede that aeroplanes are anything but second best.' His passenger's puzzlement had deepened even further. Rhodri laughed. 'Ah, I take it my aunt did not enlighten you as to her wild and wicked past.'

'No.' Wild and wicked? Thank heaven Uncle Rhys was safely on his way back to Conwy. One hint of this and he'd have taken her back too, trussed up and gagged if need be. It all sounded rather exciting.

'I suppose she doesn't talk about it much now. Everyone on the island knows about it, of course. It's what she was famous for.'

'You mean she flew in them?' Menna stared, bending her mind once more to imagining the respectable Miss Lloyd wafting about the country dangled beneath the precarious sail of a giant balloon.

'Oh yes. All the time. Drove my grandfather mad, apparently. Not literally, of course,' he added hastily. 'It was long before aeroplanes were even thought of, and it was quite the thing, you know, in those days. She preferred the speed and endurance side of the sport. Apparently she used to be seen all the time in the skies above Anglesey, and over the mainland, too. Newspaper reporters came from all over, even as far as London to cover her distance attempts. They say even Queen Victoria had heard of the *Dragonfly*.'

'The *Dragonfly*?'

'The name Aunt Gwenan gave to her balloon.'

'Doesn't she fly it any more, then?'

'Oh no. Gave up years ago. When I was a boy, in fact. To be honest with you, Miss Williams, I believe it was because she lost her nerve. At least that's what my father used to say when he was alive, and Aunt Gwenan will never talk about it. Something must have happened. I don't know what, exactly. Must have been pretty serious, though, to make Aunt Gwenan give up flying. Anyhow, she never went near the *Dragonfly* afterwards. Sad, really, that it will never fly again.'

'What happened to it?'

'What?'

'The balloon, the *Dragonfly*?'

'Oh, no idea,' he replied, lightly. 'She must have got rid of it. Out of sight, out of mind, eh.' He was concentrating on negotiating a particularly tight bend, which opened out to an ornamental iron gate, conveniently open, where a trackway led upwards towards a large house overlooking the sea. 'Here are. Bryn Hyfryd. And it is a pleasant hill, too, just as its name says, don't you think?'

Menna had to agree. As they approached the house she discovered a flat expanse of green fields stretching all around. The house itself was of stone, with more windows than Menna had ever seen in one building in her life before, while the roof gleamed with the delicate variations of green, purple, and grey slate.

On the side nearest the sea she could make out an enormous ornamental conservatory, green with the fronds of palms and ferns, leading into a garden, through which a path wound its way down towards the curving bay of a small sandy beach.

'Big, eh?' Rhodri remarked at her silence.

'Very,' Menna agreed, nervously.

'Don't worry, Miss Williams, you'll soon find it's not nearly as smart as it looks. Its been sadly neglected over the years. My aunt, I'm afraid, does not believe in throwing money around.'

Menna frowned. On the tip of the tongue was her protest that Miss Lloyd was, on the contrary, rather generous to her staff, but then she bit the words back. She had, she reminded herself, yet to see the colour of Gwenan Lloyd's money. Perhaps the promises had been empty. Perhaps the reality would be something else altogether.

Unease stirred deep in her belly. Her new employer could quite easily have lied about how much she would pay her. Once in her employ, away from her friends and with no other job to go to, it would be easy to keep Menna there by the threat of being dismissed with no references, and with no hope of getting another post at all. And, in any case, she would need to work an entire month before she found out for certain.

These unpleasant thoughts were interrupted by a drone overhead.

'It's following us.' Menna said, looking up to see the aeroplane swooping low over their heads. The next moment she gasped in alarm. 'It's coming down!' she cried, expecting the fragile little craft to smash headlong into the ground at any moment.

'Oh yes.' Rhodri was calm. 'That's its landing-strip over by the sea there. The large shed on the cliffs is its hangar.'

'Oh.' Menna watched in fascination as the aeroplane touched both wheels down on the grass, and then bounced along in a rather alarming fashion. 'That was close,' she breathed, as it swerved to a stop right on the edge of the cliff.

'Reckless idiot,' Rhodri said. He pulled the automobile up to a halt on the gravel in front of the house. 'He's always pulling stunts like that. Likes to show off,' he added, irritably. 'He'll kill himself one of these days, if he's not careful.'

Menna didn't dare ask, but fortunately Rhodri was not hesitant about any explanations. 'My brother, Tal,' he announced. 'Only thing he cares about is that 'plane of his,' Rhodri was saying. 'He's a selfish devil, though I say it

27

myself. If you'll take my advice, you'll stay well out of his way.'

Looking down, he caught the alarm in Menna's eyes. 'Don't worry,' he added, his voice softening. 'He spends most of his time tinkering with that machine of his, or off getting bits and pieces to improve it. You're not likely to come across him much.'

He jumped out of the automobile, and strode round to open the passenger door. 'Come along then, Miss Williams,' he said. 'I'll take you to my aunt.'

3

'You are late.' Miss Lloyd, it seemed, was not about to be impressed by, given the circumstances, the miracle of her being there at all.

'Yes, I'm sorry, Aunt, it's entirely my fault. Miss Williams had been waiting some time at the quay when I arrived.'

'Hmm.' Miss Lloyd's eyes matched the palest of grey slate on the roof, and at this moment there was a certain icy fire to their depths that made Menna very uneasy indeed.

'Well, I'm sure it needn't have taken that long.' At the sound of the soft voice with its quiet edge of complaint, Menna's eyes flickered towards the speaker, a tall, elegantly-dressed young woman with a veritable fountain of broderie anglaise floating delicately over the collar and cuffs of her white blouse, who was sitting in the window seat not even bothering to take a single glance towards the new housekeeper from the moment Menna and Rhodri had entered.

'Well, I'm afraid, Charlotte, that it did,' replied her fiancé with good-humoured patience.

'Well, you left me alone for hours,' Lady Charlotte complained, her full lips formed into a pout she clearly felt was irresistible to her intended. 'And with nothing to amuse me, in the least. It was unbearably tedious. I don't know why I came.'

No compassionate visiting then, it seemed. Menna studiously avoided Rhodri's eyes. That tale had obviously been for the peace of mind of her uncle as he watched her being whisked off alone by a young man who, had an unfortunately detained fiancée not carefully been brought out and dangled in front of Rhys, might have been considered to harbour all kinds of intentions.

'Well, I shall just have to be all yours

now,' Rhodri replied with a particularly dazzling smile. 'I promise we will do everything you wish to do for the rest of the day.' The pout softened a little.

'Very well then,' she said, getting to her feet and sweeping past Menna, still without a glance. 'I shall expect you to start at this moment. And you mustn't ever leave me like that again. Ever.'

With a rueful grin, Rhodri gave a small ironic bow in Menna's direction, and followed behind the elegant skirts of his intended.

Menna kept her eyes carefully on the floor. Had the bored Lady Charlotte been up since dawn like Aunt Margaret, getting the grate going and a family fed before working until dusk on the paddle steamers, an hour or so of idleness would have been a luxury, she thought to herself with irritation.

Let her take a boat out with the mussel fishermen, like many a widow was forced to do, especially when the swell was high and the wind laced with sleet, then she could complain.

Menna looked up to find Miss Lloyd watching her narrowly. Suddenly afraid that her thoughts had shown in her face, Menna felt alarm rising. She was not such a fool as to be aware just how great a catch Lady Charlotte would be for any family in the area, and any sign of rebellious opinions amongst the staff would be quickly stamped upon.

She was just in time to catch a small twitch at the side of her new employer's mouth, that could have been a nervous tick, or the hastily-smothered beginnings of amusement. The eyes, however, were just as chilly as before.

'If I were you, Miss Williams, I wouldn't even consider the matter.'

'I beg your pardon?' Miss Lloyd seemed in the habit of starting conversations halfway through, in a belief that her hearer instinctively knew the rest.

'My nephews. Handsome young men, both of them. But not a Prince Charming between them. Shut out here alone with them, a pretty girl like yourself might permit herself to dream.

I should warn you, Miss Williams, despite appearances, we are no longer a wealthy family. Unfortunately, my nephews have inherited expensive tastes and to maintain them, they will have to marry into money.

'That, as I am sure you are aware, is the way of the world. There will be no *servant makes good* in this house, and the first sign of anything, less reputable shall we say, and I shall have no hesitation in sending you packing.'

'I didn't — ' Menna began, scarlet in the face, and stumbling over her words in a sudden rush of fury. What kind of empty-headed idiot did Miss Lloyd take her for? She took a deep breath. 'I took up this post because it was an advancement, and my job at the Castle Hotel was ending for the winter months,' she replied with dignity. 'I am not looking for love, Miss Lloyd, or marriage.'

She waited for the older woman's scornful disbelief that any young woman should not be looking out for an advantageous marriage, cursing herself for not taking up that offer of a permanent position at the hotel and instead, rushing off into the power of this impossible woman. There was a moment's silence.

'I'm glad to hear it,' came Miss Lloyd's voice at last. Her tone was sharp, but mercifully lacking in contempt. 'Neither are calculated to bring happiness in my experience.'

'There are some happy marriages,' Menna shot back. She bit her lip despairingly. Why did that tongue of hers always run away with her?

'Ah, so you are a romantic after all,' Gwenan Lloyd replied with a dangerous softness.

'I didn't mean it like that.'

'And just how did you mean it, Miss Williams?' Her very chance to begin her work here hung in the balance at those tersely-spoken words. Menna could feel it. Well, at this point there was nothing to lose. Abandoning any pretence at respect, she pulled herself up to her full height, and looked her employer straight in the eye.

'I mean I have seen several long marriages, based on equality and respect, just as much as passion, where two people have worked hard to make a better life for themselves and raise a family. I wasn't thinking of a fairytale, Miss Lloyd, but of my aunt and uncle in Conwy, who have loved each other for the best part of twenty years, and also had room in their hearts for me when I needed it.'

There was a moment's silence. Even the frosty Miss Lloyd appeared to have been taken aback at quite such boldness, and quite beyond speech. Instead, Menna found a reply coming from the half-open door behind her.

'A very pretty speech. I only hope you can believe it.'

'Of course I believe it!' Stung beyond any caution, Menna swung round to confront this new source of attack. 'I wouldn't have said it otherwise.' What on earth was it with all these Lloyds?

There was no mistaking the young man in the doorway as Rhodri's brother. He had the same dark eyes, flecked with a touch of blue rather than green, and the same thick dark hair.

If she was in any doubt, she had only to look at the leather jacket he was unbuttoning with one hand, and the helmet and goggles held in the other, to recognise the pilot of the aeroplane that had followed them.

'Words are easy when it is your employment that is at stake,' he replied, cynically.

'Oh? And you'd know that, would you?' This time Menna startled even herself with her frankness. Tal Lloyd's face grew white beneath his sunburn, and his lips tightened dangerously.

Oh, well, that was it, then. And she wasn't even likely to be offered a lift to the nearest railway station, and heaven knows how far that was. Menna braced herself, and prepared to stalk out with the last of her dignity intact, leaving her belongings to be collected later. She was stopped in her tracks by an unexpected sound, a low cackle that appeared to be Miss Lloyd laughing.

'Well, I doubt if this young woman will be setting her cap at you, Tal,' she remarked. 'Almost a pity really, she might have done you some good.'

'I'm sorry — ' Menna began. If by any miracle she was about to remain here, she had no desire to make an enemy of one of the family, especially one in a position to make her life impossible.

'Don't be,' Miss Lloyd put in. 'My nephew is thick-skinned enough to hear a few truths in his life. Besides, you'll spoil the effect, and I might start doubting you again.'

'You mean I can stay?'

'Of course you are staying. When Mrs Jones retired, I had no intention of taking on any woman under the age of thirty-five, but I was impressed by your directness from the first, Miss Williams, not to mention the excellent reference from the Castle Hotel, and the fact that they clearly had no real wish to let you go. I'd have been a fool not to offer you the post there and then.'

Menna could almost have hugged her with relief. She took a deep breath and promised herself never to speak her mind again, however much she was provoked. Her future in her own photographic studio was far too precious to be put at risk by the likes of Tal Lloyd.

'Thank you, Miss Lloyd,' she murmured demurely, watching the retreating leather-clad back of the pilot out of the corner of her eye as he walked over to the window where Lady Charlotte had been sitting and stood looking out into the grounds as if the two women behind him did not exist.

Gwenan Lloyd was already on her feet, one hand on the bell-pull beside her.

'Mari will show you where everything is. It has all been rather neglected I'm afraid. Mrs Jones was not in the least well for the year before she retired and she was rather elderly. However, Miss Williams, I'm sure you'll be able to get things shipshape and organised in no time.'

'Yes, Miss Lloyd.' Menna resisted the temptation to sink to the floor in a deep curtsey, or at least kiss her new employer's feet. Anyone else, she was well aware, would have had such a troublesome prospect out on her ear before sundown.

Instead, the chill seemed to have marginally thawed from Gwenan Lloyd's pale grey eyes, and her thin face had softened a little into the faint hauntings of a wry smile. All of which, Menna realised with a jolt of surprise, added to the fact that the severe Miss Lloyd might even rather like her.

As she left, Menna took a quick glance back at her employer. She appeared small, and slight, and even rather frail in the grandiose surroundings of her home. Had she really, Menna found herself wondering, once been the intrepid adventurer Rhodri had spoken of?

Miss Lloyd had already moved to join her nephew at the window.

'And how was the sky today?' she was asking.

'Magnificent,' he replied, his tone gentler than any he had used before. 'I've hardly seen it so clear. You could see right across Snowdon, right down the coast past Barmouth. He smiled down at his aunt with unmistakable affection. 'I still think you should come with me one of these days, you know.'

'Hmm,' she grunted as if by saying neither yes or no she could sidestep an argument.

At that moment, Menna knew that everything Rhodri had told her was true. She could hear it in the hunger in the older woman's tone when she asked about Tal's flight, and in the abrupt manner, she halted any hope she would take up his offer and head for the clouds once more.

She wanted to, Menna could hear it in her voice, more than life itself. So what was it that could have happened, all those years ago? Menna asked herself. What had happened to Gwenan, or to the *Dragonfly*, to make her so determined not to fly, even when the chance was there beside her, and every part of her clearly yearned to go?

One day, Menna determined, she would find out.

4

For the next week Menna had no time to even think about the mystery of the *Dragonfly*. When Miss Lloyd had spoken of the house being neglected, she had not been exaggerating. Dust and dirt had collected in every corner, several of the curtains needed mending, and much of the furniture looked as if it hadn't been polished in years.

It seemed that while Miss Lloyd was prepared to pay her staff well, she was in no hurry to employ many of them. Menna discovered she had only the help of Mari, a shy hard-working girl of nineteen from a neighbouring village, to help her with the house and the preparing of meals for the family, with the absent Harri Jacobs doubling as gardener and general handyman.

Even at the Castle Hotel, Menna had never worked so hard in her life. The kitchens were the worst. Mrs Jones' eyesight had not been of the best, and every surface was covered in stains and a thin coating of grime, which Mari had done her best to keep to a minimum, a battle she had been constantly losing.

On her first afternoon off, therefore, Menna felt she did not have the energy to even go and explore the nearby villages. On the other hand, it was a bright day, cool and blustery, with plenty of clear sunshine and she had no wish to waste her precious free hours indoors.

'How far can you go along the beach?' she asked Mari, who was polishing some of the much-neglected silver with a yawn.

'Right along to the next headland, I think, miss, when the tide's out. A whole day's walk so my brother says. But you can walk almost to that shed thing where Mr Tal keeps his aeroplane at any time. It's nice and quiet there. It's a private beach, see, no-one goes. Miss Lloyd is out there with her stick if she spots even a boat landing there.'

'Then that's where I'll walk,' Menna said decidedly. 'I certainly couldn't walk a whole day at the moment.'

★ ★ ★

The tide was almost fully in as Menna began to walk along the sands. Damp pebbles glistened in blues and greens and the odd glow of crimson as she walked, while each wave swept bits of seaweed and the odd wriggling crab up to her feet.

A chill-edged breeze stirred the tops of breaking waves sending salt spray into her face and to cling in shining droplets in her hair.

She paused at the edge of the water, taking in deep breaths of sea air as she gazed over the seemingly endless expanse of sea in front of her.

Menna clutched the camera she had brought with her in case she should come across a scene to photograph. She would need a collection to display in the new studio, and if she asked Sam Makepeace for her prints displayed in the shop he would soon guess what she was about.

She had retrieved enough chemical solution to process several films. That was the easy part. To print them she would need a darkroom, and that would take time and money, and a suitable place . . .

She sighed. She always came back up against a brick wall of the impossibility of achieving her plans. Besides, there was so much to do at Bryn Hyfryd when would she ever find even the time or the energy to roam around the island looking for views that would make the kind of photographs that would have people stopping in amazement, and then drawn in irresistibly to purchase a print, or have their portrait taken?

It was just a dream, she told herself, a foolish dream, just to comfort herself, and not face the fact that Sam and Guto had won.

She looked over the sea once more.

From the hilltops of the mainland she had often seen the coastline of Ireland hovering on the horizon on a clear day. Beyond that, Dad had told her, it was all Atlantic Ocean, all the way to the New World of America.

Lots of people were emigrating there, she had heard, leaving the old world to make a better life for themselves in the opportunities of the new. One day, it had said in the newspapers, there might even be aeroplanes flying to and fro in only a few hours.

Menna couldn't quite believe that, but there were the great liners that crossed over in a matter of days. Having lived all his life amongst boats, Uncle Rhys was fascinated by anything that sailed. Just before she had left he'd been reading about a new liner, the largest vessel, so the reporter had declared with almost hysterical excitement, ever to float on water, which would make the journey from Southampton to New York in four days, or maybe even less.

Perhaps, thought Menna to herself,

despair growing, that was what she should save her money for instead. Stay long enough in the service of Mrs Lloyd to save for steerage passage on this *Titanic*, or one of its sister ships, and try to find a post in a photographic studio in America, far away from Guto Makepeace and his roving hands. Far away, too, from her family, and the home she loved so much . . .

'You can't leave.' Menna had never quite understood the expression about 'jumping out of your skin' until this sudden answer to her thoughts. She swung round to discover a man in a creased linen suit and broad-rimmed hat sitting in a hollow of the bank behind the beach, one hand poised, pencil at the ready, above a sketch-book on his knee.

'I'm sorry, I didn't mean to startle you.' He remained seated, although he removed his hat, revealing a thick expanse of dark hair liberally tinged with grey that reached down to his shoulders in an unfashionably wild manner. 'You are the entire lynchpin of my sketch, you see.'

'Am I?' Menna found herself intrigued rather than frightened by the sudden appearance of a strange man on the beach. There was a humorous warmth in his blue eyes that put her immediately at her ease, while his sunburned face told of travels to places of a far hotter sun than was ever found on this northern island. 'Wasn't that a little rash, making something so fleeting so important?' she enquired with a smile.

'Ah,' he replied, the edges of his eyes crinkling up in laughter, 'but I was trusting that you would be so enchanted by the scene I would have at least a few more minutes.'

Menna laughed. There was something about him that made her immediately forget her troubles, almost as if anything were possible.

'And if I remain will you allow me to see the sketch?'

'Of course.'

'Very well, then. I shall be enchanted

by the scene.' She turned back to face the sea once more.

'Mind you,' the stranger was adding, 'I'm afraid I cannot view you quite in the same light again.'

'Oh?'

'Apart from being dazzled by your beauty — '

'Naturally.'

'I now see you are one of the enemy.'

'Enemy?' Menna turned her head to frown at him. Was this one of the Lloyds' little feuds she knew nothing about?

'The camera you are holding.'

'Oh, that,' she answered, in relief.

'You may well say 'that', young woman, but 'that' is what will soon be putting painters like me out of their profession. One click of a button, a few chemicals, and there you are, endless copies of the same picture. How can we poor scribblers compete?'

'It's an entirely different thing,' Menna said. 'How can there be any competition at all? I'm sure people will always want paintings. You can use your imagination much more freely, and besides, you use colour.'

'And you don't think a process will be found to create colour photographs one day?' he responded, in mock gloom.

'And do you think only the rich should be able to have portraits of themselves?' she shot back.

'Ouch! Touché. You are quite right, of course. It is only something like photography that can be fast and mass produced that can be affordable to everyone. And at that, I think I should tell you, you can move now.'

Menna turned and walked up to where he was sitting.

'May I see?'

'Of course.' He held out the sketch. It showed the beach, and the rolling waves, and a figure Menna could just recognise as herself standing on the shore looking wistfully out to sea. Her eyes suddenly sharpened. There in the sky in the figure's line of vision, faint, almost as if the sketcher had changed his mind and used a piece of Indian rubber to remove it, was the unmistakable shape of a hot-air balloon.

'The *Dragonfly*,' Menna breathed.

'What?' Her companion looked up startled. 'What do you know about the *Dragonfly*?'

'Only that it was Miss Lloyd's, and she was famous for flying it. I'm the new housekeeper at Bryn Hyfryd,' she explained to his enquiring look.

'Are you now. So Mrs Jones has retired at last. I should have guessed, finding you on the Lloyds' private beach.' His humour had gone, and he reached for the sketch, as if regretting he had asked her to pose for him at all.

'You mean I couldn't possibly be a friend of the family, or engaged to one of Miss Lloyd's nephews,' Menna retorted, stung.

'No,' he replied, his face softening into a smile once more. 'You look far too sensible a young woman to wish to shackle yourself to either of Gwenan's nephews. Leave them to the unfortunate young ladies of the land who are rich in money, and poor in the brains that should tell them to know better.' His tone was suddenly bitter. 'I wouldn't wish a Lloyd on my worst enemy.'

'Oh.' Menna blinked, a thousand questions spinning through her mind, but before she could pull herself together to voice one she found the painter closing his sketch book and pulling himself to his feet, retrieving as he did so a finely-carved walking-stick half hidden in the sand.

'Speaking of which . . . ' he remarked, coolly, looking over her shoulder and down the length of the beach. Menna turned to find a familiar figure striding purposefully along the shore-line towards them.

★ ★ ★

'This is a private beach.' Tal Lloyd's face glowered with suppressed fury.

'Yes, yes. I am aware of that,' Menna's new friend replied.

'Then what are you doing here?'

The hand on the walking-stick grew white at the knuckles, but the stranger's voice remained calm.

'I came to paint the scene. A rather flattering reason for trespass, don't you find?'

'No, I don't find.' Tal's temper appeared to rise rather than be deflected by this touch of humour. 'And I don't want my aunt disturbed.'

'And what do you propose to do about it?' The older man stepped down from the sand dune, walking easily leaning on his walking-stick, but with a pronounced limp. 'Chase me off?'

'No, of course not.' Apparently caught off-guard, Tal hesitated, frowning, clearly at a loss what to say next.

'Good, because I'll hope you remember, Taliesin, that I've been sketching on this beach since before you were a squirt in short trousers, too young to wipe your own nose. And don't worry about Gwenan. She has made her feelings perfectly clear. I have no intentions of disturbing her.'

He turned to Menna, whose eyes were round, and whose cheeks were sucked in with the effort of not breaking out into peals of laughter at the younger man's discomfiture. 'Nice to have met you, miss, and I hope we meet again under more pleasant circumstances.'

'Me, too,' Menna murmured politely, aware of Tal's gaze transferring itself to glare at her.

'Good day to you both.' And with that, Tal's opponent was limping rapidly along the sands towards the headland farthest away from the house, sketchbook tucked neatly under one arm.

5

'And I suppose you think he's wonderful, too,' Tal snapped at her when the man was out of earshot.

'No, of course not.' Menna met his glare unblinkingly. 'Why should I? We only spoke for a few minutes.'

'So he didn't tell you he's the great David Llewelyn. I suppose you've heard of him?'

'Of course.' She'd once been to an exhibition of David Llewelyn's paintings in London, when Dad had taken her there in a vain hope of expanding his photographic portraits into the society of the rich and famous, before he'd taken on Sam Makepeace and settled down in the shop in Conwy.

A local man, he was, David Llewelyn, Dad explained. Well, local to Anglesey, which was almost the same. Lived somewhere abroad, now. Too grand for them now he was rich, and his paintings were the most sought after throughout Europe. Menna wished she had looked more closely at his sketch.

'Then I do think he's wonderful,' she added, defiantly. 'At least, I think his paintings are.' Delicate, atmospheric paintings that captured the spirit of the place more than a photograph ever could. Menna's mind dragged itself back to the present. 'Why did he call you Taliesin?'

'That's my name.'

'You mean after the bard in the Mabinogion stories?'

'Yes,' he growled.

'Oh.'

'What?'

'Nothing.'

'Nothing, I suspect, is never nothing with you, Miss Williams.'

'I just didn't see you as a druidic bard strumming a harp,' she replied, before she could stop herself.

'I see.' His voice was dangerously quiet. 'But?'

'I beg your pardon?'

'I can feel a 'but' coming on.'

'Oh, nothing.'

'Nothing?'

'Well, I was just going to say that I expect your mother could. See you as a bard, that is,' she added, hastily. Well, if that didn't have him striding down the beach in a fine temper nothing would. To her astonishment he let out a grunt that could possibly have been a stifled laugh.

'So that's why she was always placing crowns of mistletoe on my head,' he replied, with a smile.

Now Menna was used to smiles, people smiled at her camera lens all the time. She was, she felt, quite impervious to smiles. Which is why this one caught her by surprise, and off her guard. It was a wide, charming smile that quite unexpectedly set her treacherous heart racing. She rather wished he'd return to glaring. There was a moment's silence, 'And so what were you and David Llewelyn finding to talk so earnestly about?'

'Mmm? Oh, nothing.' She met his raised brows. 'Only photography,' she said, casually, feeling this was a sufficiently uninteresting subject to anyone whose only real passion appeared to be flying around in aeroplanes.

'Photography. You know about photography?' This was clearly not to be Menna's day.

'A little,' she replied, warily.

'Of course, Aunt said you'd worked for Makepeace & Williams before the hotel.'

'Williams & Makepeace,' she retorted angrily. 'And I didn't work for anybody. I am Williams.'

'Are you now.' His attention was now full upon her, with an intensity Menna wasn't quite sure she liked. His eyes strayed down her form, not to admire the proportions of her figure, but to rest on the camera held in her hand. 'Well I wish you'd tell Makepeace to buck up his ideas, he'll be running you both out of business if he carries on like this.'

'It's not my business any more,' she replied, humiliated by the admission.

'Well you must be part of it if your name is still on the door. If Mr Makepeace has taken the trouble to change around the names on the sign I don't doubt he'd be the kind to get rid of his partner's name if he was able.'

'He may not be able to get rid of the partnership, but he certainly got rid of me,' she snapped, alarmed to find herself so close to tears. She'd never told anyone this before, not even Uncle Rhys and Aunt Margaret, not in so many words. Not bleakly, and inescapably like this. So why was she telling this ill-tempered man who had clearly despised her from the moment they met?

'I see.'

She looked up to meet his dark eyes watching her, the blue suddenly prominent, softening the harshness of his gaze. 'But he can't do that legally, not without your agreement. There are laws to protect you.'

'Laws mean a lawyer, and a lawyer costs money. Where do you think I'm going to get that kind of money from?'

'So you're just going to give up.'

'No, of course not. I'm going to start up on my own.' Alarm rushed through her. She had said too much, revealed herself as a non-too-loyal employee who would leave the first opportunity that arose . . .

'Are you now.' He was watching her horribly closely. Menna swallowed. And this was not, she told herself sharply, the time to notice the strong lines of his high cheekbones, or the wide curve of his mouth, which were somehow managing to disrupt the rhythm of her breathing, and turning the depths of her belly into mush. 'So are you looking for commissions?'

'I beg your pardon?'

'Well, Miss Williams, either you are or you aren't.'

'But I'm already employed.'

'I had noticed.'

'By your aunt,' she reminded him,

acidly. 'I can hardly start taking myself off from my duties to work for somebody else.'

'Mmm.' He considered this. Now, perhaps, Menna prayed, he would leave her alone, and her heartbeat could start getting back to normal.

'If you'll excuse me, Mr Lloyd . . . '

'Supposing it was for her benefit.'

'What?'

'Supposing the commission was for my aunt's benefit. How would you feel, then?'

'I, er — ' He'd got her. Trapped. Even Menna wasn't fool enough to think there wasn't an unmistakable hunger in her own eyes at the thought of getting back to the work she loved. 'I haven't got any materials. Or a darkroom,' she protested, feebly.

'I'll provide them. And I'll pay you for your time.' He saw her mouth open again. 'And I promise it will not interfere with your work in the house. A small commission, that's all it is. And, if my idea takes off, with more to follow later.'

'What kind of commission?'

'Landscapes. Castles. Mountains. Beaches. The kind of thing tourists would like.'

'I can take landscapes.'

'Well these have to be special ones. And it's no good glaring at me like that, miss, I'm not saying you can't take special photographs. Judging by some I saw when that idiot, Makepeace, was wittering on I'd say you can take very special photographs. These are just to be special because of the angle from which they are to be taken.'

For a moment Menna looked at him blankly, then horrified realisation dawned.

'Oh, no you don't. No! Count me out. Find someone else. No.'

'Funny,' he replied, calmly. 'All the photographers I've approached say that.'

'Because they're not totally insane, of course,' she replied.

'You'll be perfectly safe.'

'No!'

'You mean you don't trust me?'

'That's not fair.'

'I've flown that thing for miles, and been caught in all weathers, and never had to make an emergency landing yet.' He caught her sceptical gaze. 'All right. One. But that was when I was just starting. I'm a good pilot, you know. I wouldn't put you in any danger.'

'Danger?' Menna heard herself squeak. 'You expect me to sail up above the highest mountain in nothing more than a wooden box with wings, and you tell me that's not dangerous!'

'I can think of more dangerous things.'

'You mean like a hot-air balloon?' she said, suddenly feeling rather small, and cowardly. Miss Lloyd had been up plenty of times in a hot-air balloon at the mercy of the air currents.

'So Rhodri told you about that.' His eyes were suddenly sharp. 'Yes, Menna, like a hot-air balloon. At least I have an engine to keep me in the air and let me control where I am going.'

'I suppose.' Menna swallowed. This felt like signing her life away. And yet there was a part of her that would love to see what it was like, flying amongst the clouds, just once, even if it was the last thing she ever did. And strangely enough, she realised, she did trust him. How, or why, she could not have said, unless it was that smile she had glimpsed directed towards his aunt, as if he would never let anything harm her. 'All right. I'll do it,' she shot out, before she could think about this and regret it.

'Good. I thought someone who's not afraid of speaking their mind wouldn't be stopped by a little thing like flight.'

'I must be mad,' she muttered to herself. Maybe she didn't trust him. Maybe she just felt like that because he made her insides go all peculiar, and this was the worst decision she had ever made in her life . . .

'So, are you ready?'

'What!'

'It's your afternoon off, isn't it? I take it that's why you're wandering the

64

countryside talking to stray artists. Now's as good a time as any.'

'Now?'

'Yes. Now. Any reason why not?'

She swallowed hard.

'I take it there's film in that thing.'

'Some. Not a lot,' she added, hopefully.

'That'll do. This can be a trial run.'

Menna took a deep breath. Oh well, better now than have it hanging over her all week like an execution.

'I hope it doesn't hurt, much, when we fall out of the sky,' she muttered gloomily to herself. 'Well, what are we waiting for?' was all she said aloud, turning to follow his rapid steps towards the shed where the aeroplane was waiting.

'Mr Lloyd?' she ventured as they left the beach and made their way up a steep path to the shed. 'Can I ask you something?'

'If you wish,' he replied, coolly.

'David Llewelyn — ' At the name her companion stopped in his tracks, and frowned down at her.

'Yes?'

'How did he know about the *Dragonfly*?'

'The *Dragonfly*?'

'Yes. He'd put it in his sketch, flying above the ocean with someone watching it.'

'You, I take it?'

'Yes. I didn't mind, and he was very polite. Only — ' She hesitated.

'Yes?'

'He seemed to have changed his mind. About the *Dragonfly*, I mean. It looked as if he'd decided to take it out of the picture altogether.'

'Oh.' He gave her such a searching look she found herself almost beginning to squirm. 'And Rhodri didn't tell you that part?'

'No, why should he? We only talked in the car on the way here.' Why on earth had Tal seemed to have got it into his head that she knew his brother far better than either of them was letting on? Menna felt herself turning scarlet to the roots of her hair. 'Tal Lloyd, you don't think — you can't possibly believe that Rhodri was the one who made sure I came here?'

'It had crossed my mind. It has been done before with a couple of the maids, until Mrs Jones put her foot down and found Mari. Rhodri always could twist Aunt Gwenan round his little finger,' he added, a trifle bitterly.

'But with his fiancée there visiting — '

'Don't be naïve,' he snapped.

Menna's temper hit the roof of her head. 'And don't you be stupid,' she growled. 'Do I look like the kind of girl who would, well, carry on like that with someone who was certain to drop me like a brick the moment he became bored?'

Suddenly, she was floundering. She wouldn't be surprised if her entire head of hair had acquired the colour of the heat in her face. It had suddenly dawned on her that she felt she could quite easily become that kind of girl, given the right circumstances, and the right circumstances were standing alarmingly close at this moment.

'No.' Thank heaven he did not appear to read her thoughts, and merely took her confusion for a young woman's natural embarrassment. 'I should have known it the moment I saw you that first day with Aunt Gwenan.' His smile was apologetic, and quite alarmingly charming. 'Rhodri, I'm afraid, has a taste for the more docile species of womanhood. Though I'm not sure he wasn't a little blinded when he decided on the woman rich enough to be his wife.'

Menna found her mouth twitching in response. Lady Charlotte's whine might sound like appealing weakness to a young man, but Menna had come across enough spoilt young women in her studio to be able to recognise the potential for some spectacular tantrums beneath that soft exterior.

'Good.' She smiled in acceptance of the apology. 'So, David Llewelyn?' She asked, feeling a need to draw the conversation back on to safer ground.

'Ah, David Llewelyn. When I was a boy he used to visit all the time. He was engaged to be married to my aunt.'

'Really?' Handsome, talented, gentlemanly David Llewelyn wanting to marry the cold-eyed Miss Lloyd? Menna found her mouth had dropped open, and shut it quickly.

'She was besotted with him, apparently. But something happened. He let her down badly, I believe. Then he married someone else and moved abroad to fame and fortune. Aunt Gwenan never forgave him. Everyone says her troubles started from there.'

'I'm sorry.' She could understand some of the bitterness in Miss Lloyd's face. Whatever he had done, to have lost someone like David Llewelyn . . .

'I'd heard he was back, of course.' Tal resumed his way up the path. 'His wife died last year. He moved back to Anglesey a few months ago. He'd just better not get any ideas about getting back in touch with Aunt Gwenan, that's all. He's done enough damage in my book. If he does try it'll be over my dead body.'

'Oh,' Menna said. From the fierceness in his voice she was in no doubt that he meant it. Any other time and she might have questioned him more, but looming up above was a sight that made her heart grow cold, and all other considerations scurry right out of her head.

'Here we are, then,' Tal said, suddenly cheerful, David Llewelyn dismissed from his considerations. 'It won't take me a moment to get her ready, then we shall be up in the air in a moment.'

6

'Are you all right there? If you feel sick at all there's a container just down by your feet.'

'No!' Menna yelled, above the roar of the wind. Gingerly, she opened her eyes. How on earth she came to be wedged inside a small box, with Tal's disembodied voice somewhere near, wings either side of her, and nothing else but air between her and oblivion, she could not have said.

'We're crossing the Menai Straights,' Tal called. 'They look beautiful from up here.'

'I'm sure they do,' Menna muttered to herself. It was looking at them at all that was the problem. Oh well, this was supposed to be for her to take photographs, so she'd better give it a try. Just a quick one, mind.

She took a brief peer through her

goggles over the side of her little compartment. It looked very far away down there. Very small. Telford's Menai suspension bridge looked like a toy, and the ships making their way up and down seemed even smaller.

'I can't do this,' she shrieked inside, shutting her eyes once more, swearing she'd never open them again until they were safely back on the ground.

'We're coming up on Conwy!' came Tal's voice, cutting through her terror.

'Are we?' Despite everything, this was something she couldn't resist. She opened her eyes, slowly. 'Oh my goodness,' she gasped.

'Isn't it magnificent?'

'You can see all the town!' The fact that she was suspended in mid-air with no visible support to keep her there escaped Menna's mind instantly. 'All the castle, and the walls.' It looked just like a fairy-tale town, straight from a book. The high towers of the castle overlooking the sea, and the little town behind it kept safe within its encircling stone walls punctuated by small turrets.

A train chugged slowly past in a cloud of steam and disappeared into the bridge over the river where it met the sea. 'I can see the boats!' she cried, excitedly, as her eyes travelled up the river. Down below her, chugging away towards the castle and the bridge, a little paddle-steamer churned through the water taking its last load of passengers back to Conwy after a visit to the Roman Spa halfway up the valley.

Wait until she told Uncle Rhys about this! Not that he'd ever believe her . . . 'The photographs!' she remembered, rather belatedly. Already they were soaring up the river and on towards the mountains.

'Not to worry,' Tal replied, 'I'll take her round again.'

'Thanks.' Menna tore her unwilling eyes away from the scene laid out below her, and forced herself to concentrate on the camera on her lap. She had never tried anything like this before, and it would take all her powers of concentration to get anything like a half decent picture. And half decent wasn't enough. Not any more.

'Ready?' Tal called. They had banked round and were out over the sea again, coming up on the town and castle laid out below them.

'Ready,' Menna returned, grasping her camera firmly.

* * *

'Well?' Tal Lloyd swung himself easily down from the aeroplane, and watched in amusement as his passenger slid, less than gracefully, down the side to land on the grass behind him.

'That was wonderful,' Menna gasped, struggling with her helmet. 'Did you see the train on Snowdon?' she demanded, as he bent to help her with the buckle.

'Stand still for a moment,' he commanded as he attempted to release her, but Menna was too excited to even hear him.

74

'I could see the smoke from its funnel as it reached the ridge. And the climbers on top. And the lake below the summit. And all those mountains.' Despite her wriggling he had undone the buckle, and she pulled off the helmet and goggles. 'That was the best thing I've ever done. Ever.'

Tal grinned. Her hair was wild, and her face was flushed, and her eyes were sparkling in a way he'd never seen them before. All in all, standing so close, it was just too tempting . . .

But Menna had already turned away from him, and was reaching inside the plane. 'My camera!' she exclaimed, 'I nearly forgot.'

'Of course.' It was probably for the best, he reflected. However tempting, it just wouldn't do, under the circumstances. And, besides, this was a business arrangement. Even though at this moment he would dearly like to forget all business arrangements. 'Did you manage to get any?'

'I think so.' She bit her lip, anxiously.

'I took all the film, but I'm not sure how they'll come out. It was quite hard to hold it steady.'

'Of course, it would be.' Tal put aside temptation, and put his mind to practicalities. 'I should have thought of that. That 'plane can shake like the blazes.' He thought for a moment. 'Would a kind of bracket help, so you can attach it to the side?'

'I should think so.'

'Right. I'll get something sorted out for next time.'

'Next time?'

'Of course. Didn't you enjoy yourself?'

'Oh yes. Only, supposing the photographs don't come out?'

'Then we'll try again. And again, until they do.'

'Oh.' Menna hesitated. 'Tal, I mean, Mr Lloyd — '

'Tal is fine. The formalities sound a little foolish when you're both risking your lives amongst the clouds, don't you think? Just so long as you don't dare call me anything of the sort in front of Aunt Gwenan. She would get the wrong idea immediately, have us both skinned alive.'

'Me more than you,' Menna said, ruefully. She found those dark eyes watching her intently, and felt a blush rising. 'I mean,' she added hastily, 'I would certainly lose my job.' Just in case he got the wrong idea. Or the right idea. And Menna had a sneaking feeling it wouldn't take much on his part to make her putty in his hands, and that would not do her plans for the future any good at all.

'Ah, yes. Of course.' Tal cleared his throat. 'And if you dare call me Taliesin I shall skin you alive,' he added, lightly, easing the tension that suddenly seemed to be enveloping them both. Menna giggled. 'Now, you were asking?'

'Oh, yes. That. The photographs. What are they for? Why are they so important.'

He looked at her. She wasn't the housekeeper now, demure as she could be, and minding her tongue, she was the independent business woman striking a deal, and prepared to walk away if she felt in the least bit compromised. And it suited her.

Tal swallowed. He was going to have to be on his guard or this could end in disaster for both of them. He'd not turned a hair at Charlotte Wynn fluttering her soft eyelashes at him before settling for the younger Lloyd brother — that kind of young woman had no attraction for him. But this kind, the dishevelled, bright-eyed outspoken kind, who could go up terrified in an aeroplane and come down all shining, as if she could take on the entire world.

'They are for tourists,' he said, abruptly.

'Tourists? I thought they said they were to help Miss Lloyd.'

'So they are. The truth is that my aunt will have to find some kind of income from Bryn Hyfryd or she won't be able to afford to keep on living there.'

'Oh.' Menna digested this. 'But — '

'But there must have been money at some time?' She nodded. 'Well you're right, there was. There still is. The trouble is Gwenan can't touch it.' He sighed. 'It all comes back to the *Dragonfly*, you see. My grandfather didn't approve of Gwenan flying all over the place, he thought she should be marrying well and producing babies. He was a true Victorian, I'm afraid,' he added apologetically.

'Plenty of people still think that now.'

'I know. But now there's all this fuss about women's rights, and getting you the vote. There was nothing like that when my aunt was young.'

'Oh. So what happened? About the money, I mean.'

'Grandfather swore he'd cut her out of his will if she didn't stop 'disgracing him' as he put it, and my aunt swore she didn't want his money anyhow, if that was the condition. Then David Llewelyn came on the scene and she was all ready to go off with him.

'I think my grandfather must have got cold feet — she was his only daughter, after all — anyhow, he said he would change his mind if she could prove how good she was. A kind of bet.' Tal grinned. 'Which actually made him look a bit silly because all the papers, and Queen Victoria herself, knew exactly how good she was.'

'What was the bet?'

'That she would fly single-handedly right round the coast of Anglesey.'

'Oh.' That sounded rather tame to Menna's ears, and Tal seemed to agree.

'Grandfather should have read the newspapers,' he said. 'She was preparing to fly across the Pyrenees at the time, and there was talk of an attempt to fly round the world. Or maybe he just wanted an easy way to save face.'

'So she did it?'

'No. It was all David Llewelyn's doing — the fool insisted on helping with the ascent, and his foot got caught in the ropes that had moored the balloon to the ground. He was dragged along, and badly damaged his leg. Gwenan refused to go through with it.'

'But surely she could have tried again? They couldn't have expected her just to leave him there.'

'Oh yes. I believe Grandfather was quite reasonable about it. Gwenan nursed Llewelyn until he was back on his feet. Then the ungrateful hound abandoned her.'

'He couldn't have done!' Menna looked at him, horrified. She'd liked David Llewelyn the moment she saw him. She couldn't believe such treachery of him.

'People aren't always as they first seem, you know, Menna. He left her, everyone agrees, and married someone else almost immediately. Gwenan never flew again. Grandfather died shortly afterwards. Too soon to change his will, it seemed. My father was working for the consulate in India at the time, so Grandfather had left Gwenan the house, but no money to maintain it.

'The bet still stands, unless she can

fly the *Dragonfly* right around the island she can't touch a penny. Very nice for me and Rhodri when she dies, of course, we'll inherit the lot, but that's not the point.'

He sighed. 'So that is why I want to get tourists, and anyone else who is prepared to pay, to go up for tours around Snowdonia and Anglesey in my aeroplane. It's never been done before, and people love a novelty. They'll be flocking to Bryn Hyfryd, just to tell their friends they've been up in an aeroplane. We'll make a fortune, mark my words. And your photographs will be just the thing to tempt them in.'

'Oh,' Menna said. 'And I thought you were trying to tempt Miss Lloyd back into the air again.' He didn't reply. 'Tal, you devious devil, you are, aren't you?'

'Perhaps that is part of it. I once went up with her in the *Dragonfly* you know, during a holiday here when I was a boy. It changed my life, got me hooked on flying. I've been trying to get her to come up with me one day. I know she'd love it.'

'A pity about the *Dragonfly*, then,' Menna sighed.

'In what way?'

'Then she can't fly it again and win the bet. Not that I want you to lose your inheritance,' she added, hastily. She found Tal looking thoughtful.

'Well maybe she can,' he said slowly. He grabbed her hand. 'Come with me, but you are not to breathe a word of this to a soul.'

He strode to the shed, with Menna scurrying to keep up with him. He unlocked it, and they went inside. 'Over here.'

In the gloom, lit only by streaks of light streaming between the boards of the walls and the roof, he led her over to a small door at the far end. This one was double locked.

Quickly Tal undid them, and ushered Menna inside. There, on its own, in a small room Menna found herself confronted by a large wicker basket. A multitude of ropes lay sprawled around, and in the midst of it billowed a vast array of fine silk. It did not need the nameplate on the side of the basket to tell Menna what it was.

'The *Dragonfly*,' she whispered.

'Yes. I found it in one of the outbuildings when Rhodri and I first moved back to live here after our parents died and Aunt Gwenan took us in. It was half rotten, and it looked as if someone had tried to set it on fire.'

'No! Who could do such a thing to something so beautiful?'

'Well, a lot of people would say me, if I had any sense, and wanted to ensure Rhodri and I were richer than our wildest dreams for the rest of our lives. The bet still stands, and Bryn Hyfryd would absorb quite a bit of that money if Gwenan ever took it into her head to take it up again.'

'Oh.' Menna looked at him sideways. 'A lot of aeroplanes.'

'And automobiles,' he added, sharply. 'Why do you think Lady Charlotte puts up with such an unfashionable place to visit? Her side of the Wynn family are not quite as rich as they used to be, Aunt Gwenan's money will do very nicely to set her up in a fashionable town house in London, for a start.'

'Oh, I see,' Menna said.

'Charlotte might not miss Bryn Hyfryd if Gwenan has to sell and move to a terraced house in Beaumaris. I think she would view the change as an improvement. But this is Gwenan's home. I know she tries to make out she's a tough old stick, but she's not really. I think she keeps up that pretence so no one can get hear to her and hurt her.'

His face set in determination. 'And I'm not letting anyone do that, most of all David Llewelyn. It would kill her to move into town, she's used to wide open spaces and no-one to watch her and make sure she wears the right clothes and attends the right parties — what?' he demanded, finding Menna watching him intently.

'Nothing,' she said hastily. The fact that she was going weak at the knees again was none of his business. Well, it was since he was causing it, but it shouldn't be. 'So why are you keeping it locked away here?' she asked. 'Wouldn't Miss Lloyd be more likely to be tempted if she could see the *Dragonfly* every day and be reminded of all her flights.'

'Maybe.' His face set. 'I did try that at first. I even took it into one of the rooms of the house under the pretence of mending it. Only . . . ' His voice trailed off.

'Only?' Menna prompted, gently.

'Only somebody is determined Gwenan will never make a flight in the *Dragonfly*, ever again. See — ' he lifted up the silk fold of the balloon. Menna gasped as the movements of his hands revealed long slits cut into the material. 'And there had been an attempt to drag the basket out into the garden. Thank heaven it's so heavy, one of the servants heard something in the night and went to investigate.

'Whoever it was had the french windows open and the basket halfway through. There was a can of petrol next to the window, the aim had clearly been to set the *Dragonfly* alight. And then, you see, the bet could never have been won. There would have never been another flight of the *Dragonfly*. Ever.'

7

If only she had a darkroom! The thought ate at Menna as she resumed the cleaning and the dusting of Bryn Hyfryd that week. She had developed the film with her small store of chemicals, and the tiny pictures tantalised her with their promise of beautiful prints.

A few looked blurred, one was blank, where she knew the plane had banked suddenly leaving her pointing at empty sky, but whether the rest were in focus or full of shake, it was impossible to tell until she had the equipment to enlarge them, and turn them into prints.

A few days after their flight, Tal had taken his 'plane over the mainland to Chester, in search, so he claimed to Rhodri and his aunt as Menna helped to serve breakfast that morning, of parts for the 'plane.

'Oh, this and that,' he'd answered to Rhodri's enquiry. 'You know what these machines are like. I've a few adjustments need making, that sort of thing.'

'But I promised Charlotte you'd take her up to see a view of the Island.'

'Well then you'll just have to unpromise her, Rhodri, won't you. Maybe you should have checked with me first.'

'But you can go to Chester at any time. It can't be anything serious, or you'd be taking the automobile. Surely you can wait a few days.'

'Sorry. This is a perfect spell of weather for flying, little brother. You can allow me to impress your lady-friend on another day.'

His eyes were carefully avoiding travelling anywhere near Menna's direction. 'These are things I want to do as soon as possible,' he announced. Menna knew exactly what he meant, a bracket for the camera for their next attempt, and the equipment to set up a small darkroom in one of the outhouses.

That was two days ago. He wasn't expected back until after the weekend, but the house felt strangely empty without him. Rhodri spent much of his time driving Lady Charlotte about to see the sights, to make up for the lack of the promised aeroplane trip.

Miss Lloyd kept herself to herself as ever, working in her garden, or reading in her room. She seemed preoccupied, several times leaving her meals untouched, and starting when spoken to.

'I hope you don't mind, Miss Lloyd . . . ' Menna began hesitantly, on the Friday morning.

'What is it?' Gwenan Lloyd looked up from snipping the bud from the late-flowering roses.

'I promised to go to Conwy to see my uncle and aunt tomorrow.'

Menna wasn't sure if the older woman had remembered this arrangement for her day off. 'I'll be back on Sunday morning,' she added. 'Mari can easily cope, especially with Mr Tal not due back until Monday.'

'Yes, yes of course.' The icy tone had not wavered, but now Menna thought she could see the fragility of the woman beneath her hard shell. 'Yes, of course. You go, Miss Williams. You deserve a day away from this place. You've worked hard. In this short time you've transformed it.'

There was a touch of regret in the voice, and the grey eyes were bleak. 'I shall be sorry to see the roses end,' she added, abruptly. Almost, thought Menna, as if she knew, deep in her heart, she would not be here to see them bloom again.

'They're very beautiful,' she said.

'My sister, the boys' mother, planted these.' The edge of the voice was harder than ever, brittle almost, as if it were near to cracking. 'She loved this place. Hated leaving it for a hot, dusty climate like India. She was never strong afterwards.

'I'm sorry,' Menna said, gently.

The older woman twitched her

shoulders impatiently, as if shrugging off anything approaching a soft emotion.

'Why should you be? You've your entire life ahead of you. You don't want to be dwelling on the sorrows of people long gone.'

'I don't like to see unhappiness,' Menna replied.

The other cackled a bitter laugh in reply. 'That's because you're young,' she said. 'You'll find plenty of unhappiness as you grow older, and there's nothing you can do about it.'

'Nothing?'

Miss Lloyd looked up with suspicion in her eyes at Menna's probing tone. 'Nothing,' she replied, shortly. 'Nothing at all.'

★ ★ ★

Menna was glad to leave the house the next morning. An even more oppressive gloom seemed to have descended there during the night.

Miss Lloyd seemed to be shutting

herself away, even from Rhodri who could always charm a smile out of her.

Almost, thought Menna, uneasily, as if she had already resigned herself to the poky terrace in Beaumaris, and living her life in tiny rooms and a patch of garden. Maybe all Tal's efforts were too late, after all.

She stepped down the stairs with relief, and made her way rapidly towards the stables, where Harri Jacobs, returned from his mercy mission to his sister in Holyhead, had been primed to take her to the station.

'A penny for them.' She looked as Rhodri's voice broke in on her thoughts, and found him leaning idly against the bonnet of his automobile.

'I beg your pardon?'

'You looked as if you were putting the world to rights.' His smile broke through. 'I was hoping I might be included.'

'Do you need to be put to rights, Mr Lloyd?'

'I find we could all do with a bit of

that, don't you think?' he returned, smile broadening. 'Even my brother.' Menna frowned at the teasing quality of his tone. 'I take it you enjoyed your flight with him, Miss Williams?'

'I — ' she stumbled, caught off guard, and not at all sure what to say. Had Tal meant to include his brother when he said he didn't want anyone to know about the photographs, and his plan to save Bryn Hyfryd? And without knowing that she had been there as an employee . . . well, Menna could see how it looked.

'Yes, very much,' she managed, at last, trying to sound as casual as possible. 'It was very kind of him to take me.' At this Rhodri snorted.

'In my experience, Menna, Tal doesn't do anything without it being very much for his own good.' To which, she found, she had nothing to say.

'Will you tell Miss Lloyd?' she asked, heart sinking. If he did tell his aunt then there was no point in her returning here. And if he was intending to use his knowledge as blackmail to persuade her to give him the favours he obviously thought she was giving so freely to his brother — Menna clenched her fists. Well, then he had another think coming, and the sooner she was out of here the better.

'No, of course not. It was only by chance I saw you getting into his 'plane. What Aunt Gwen doesn't know doesn't hurt her.'

'Thank you,' Menna said, warily, not certain just how much gratitude he was expecting her to express.

'No need to thank me. And no, I don't want anything from you, if that's what you're thinking. My, you do have a suspicious mind, don't you,' he added, as a scarlet glow suffused her face. 'I don't wish you any harm. Quite the opposite, in fact. I enjoyed our little journey here.'

A rueful expression came over his face. 'I'm afraid my family duty to raise the Lloyd fortune rather overcomes certain choices, were I free to choose for myself.' He took a step closer, and grasped one hand. 'Menna — ' he began earnestly. But the next moment the sound of horses hooves and the rattle of a cart had him jumping away from her just as Harri Jacobs came into view.

Rhodri bent as if to help her with her overnight bag, his face hidden from the gardener's view. 'Be careful, Menna,' he said, in a low voice. 'Tal can be very charming when he wants to be. He has some idea he is going to solve all Aunt Gwen's problems, and then she'll shower him with gifts, when the only person who can do that is herself.'

He straightened up, and looked her directly in the eye. 'And Tal is not fussy what harm he does, so long as he gets his own way. I take it he forgot to mention the reason Aunt Gwen had to go to the mainland to find new staff was the — ah, shall we say, trouble, there has been with several of the female employees here. No, I thought he hadn't,' he added, as he saw her start.

'He likes to tell people it was all down to me. Irresponsible younger brother, and all that. Just don't be dazzled by him, Menna, or heaven knows where that may lead.'

'Ready, miss?' Harri Jacobs was pulling up beside them.

'Yes, thank you,' she murmured as Rhodri helped her into the seat next to the gardener, and handed up her bag.

'Have a pleasant time with your family, Miss Williams,' Rhodri said, calmly, as if his hurried warning had never taken place.

'I'm sure I shall, Mr Lloyd,' she returned, with equal formality, swiftly pushing down the cold pit in the middle of her stomach. 'And thank you for your help.'

And then she was gone, down the drive and through the gates, and out on to the winding roads that led towards the start of her journey home.

★   ★   ★

'You're quiet, Menna, nothing wrong is there?' Aunt Margaret asked, eyeing her niece narrowly.

'No, no. Nothing. I'm just tired, that's all, there's been so much work at Bryn Hyfryd getting the house straight.

'I see.' Margaret Williams had her own views on the matter after her husband's concerned mutterings about handsome young men and their automobiles, but she kept her thoughts to herself, and resumed her task of chopping vegetables for the family's evening meal.

Menna stirred the stew suspended over the fire in the iron grate in an absent manner. She couldn't have told Aunt Margaret what was troubling her exactly, she was not quite sure herself.

How could either of the Lloyd brothers be on her mind at all? Neither of them could possibly have any serious interest in their housekeeper, so it wasn't even worth thinking about. She'd had fun up in the aeroplane with Tal, and he'd asked her to take a few photographs. That was all. A business arrangement, to help his aunt, or so he said. Maybe even that was a lie. And it wasn't as though she hadn't been warned about him.

Her head was close to bursting with the impossibility of it all. There was Tal warning her against Rhodri, and now Rhodri warning her against Tal. Not to mention their aunt warning her against looking twice at either of them. Not that she would, of course. She was a sensible young woman, and she knew exactly what men of their class were after from girls like her, and love, let alone marriage, were not a part of it.

Menna pulled herself together. How Guto Makepeace would gloat if she became entangled with one of the Lloyd brothers and ended up an unmarried mother, and the disgrace of the town.

No, the only thing to do was to keep herself to herself and to have as little to do with either brother as possible. Work hard and save what she could, and cling to that dream of starting up her own studio, so that she would at least have the means of supporting herself. The business arrangement with Tal would help her get started. She had to see it that way.

Menna grimaced. She'd caught the looks Lady Charlotte sent him under her lashes as soon as Rhodri's attention was distracted elsewhere. Tal, it seemed had a way of attracting women whether his brother's insinuations about trouble with the maids at Bryn Hyfryd were true or not.

Having made this resolution not to become entangled with anything to do with any Lloyd existing on the face of the earth, Menna was turning to set about helping Aunt Margaret with vegetable preparation with a vengeance, when there was a knock at the door.

'Strange,' Aunt Margaret said, wiping her hands on her apron, 'you're not expecting anyone are you, Menna?'

'No,' Menna said, telling herself

firmly that her heart hadn't set about any unreasonable thumping at all.

'Must be a tradesman, then, or one of the neighbours.' Margaret went to open the door, leaving her niece hovering behind the kitchen door, cursing herself for being such a coward. It was with a sense of doom that she heard a man's voice answering her aunt at the door. There was a moment's exchange, and then the sound of footsteps moving through into the parlour at the front of the house.

'She's just here, she'll be with you in a moment,' she heard Margaret's voice, and the next moment she was confronted by her aunt, with a decided air of speculation in her eyes. 'A visitor for you, Menna,' she said.

'For me?'

'Yes.' Aunt Margaret looked just a little uneasy. 'I see you are moving in exalted circles now,' she remarked dryly.

'No, of course not, Aunt. I expect he's just being polite.' Menna smoothed her hair with the most casual gesture she could manage under the circumstances of Aunt Margaret's eagle eye watching her every move, took a deep breath, and sailed into the parlour with all the dignity she could muster.

To her surprise, she discovered that there were, in fact, two visitors waiting for her in Aunt Margaret's carefully-polished best room. Margaret Williams had clearly been far too overcome by the alarming circumstances of a well-dressed and extremely handsome gentleman calling upon her niece to mention the elegant young woman at his side.

'Miss Williams, I hope you don't mind this intrusion.'

'Not at all, Mr Llewelyn,' Menna began formally, and then immediately forgot her manners. 'How on earth did you know I was here?'

'Detective work,' he replied with a grin. 'Though not of the most arduous,' he added, as his companion placed the tip of her umbrella in a warning manner on his shoe. 'After all, there are not many housekeepers at Bryn Hyfryd who are also photographers. I'm afraid it only took the briefest of enquiries at our lodgings.'

He launched a disarmingly apologetic smile in her direction. 'My daughter, as you can see from her disapproving look, feels we should have given you some warning rather than just appearing like this. Given you the option to be out, so to speak.'

'Don't, Papa, you are embarrassing Miss Williams,' replied the young woman, pressing the umbrella rather more firmly into the leather of his boot. She turned back to Menna with a smile that, if possible, quite outdid her father's in its ability to charm. 'I'm sorry, Miss Williams, as you can see he is quite impossible to take out into polite society.'

'Not at all,' Menna said, intrigued.

Miss Llewelyn was sporting a green velvet coat that even Menna could recognise as one of the finest money could buy, while her hat appeared to have come out of the latest fashion magazine. Her voice, however, was warm, with a touch of a European accent Menna could only guess was French, and frankness and good humour glowed from her light green eyes.

'I'm Claudia Llewelyn, Miss Williams. To tell you the truth, I'm the reason we're here. I am looking for a photographer. A really good photographer. I've tried several in Bangor and Caernarfon, but they are not what I am looking for. I was impressed by the portraits in the local studio here, but I was told that particular photographer had left some time ago, and I was not tempted by their more recent work.

'Then my father mentioned he'd met you, and you seemed exactly what I was looking for. Those are your work in the window of *Makepeace and Williams*?'

'*Williams and Makepeace*,' Menna said, unable to help herself. 'Yes, they are.' Father and daughter smiled at each other, while Aunt Margaret blinked.

'I'll make the tea,' she muttered, retreating to the kitchen.

'So would you consider taking on a commission?' Claudia asked.

'What kind of a commission, Miss Llewelyn?'

'Spoken like a true business woman. And don't let her beat you down in price either.'

'Papa! You promised to stay out of this.'

'I'm just ensuring fair play,' he returned, good humouredly, retreating to a corner and taking out his sketch pad.

'I am looking for a photographer who can take pictures of women's fashion,' Claudia resumed.

'Fashion?' That had been the last thing in Menna's mind.

'Yes. When we lived in Paris I worked for a fashion house there. When we decided to move back here I decided to set up my own business.'

'I'm not sure . . . ' Menna looked at her elegant form uncertainly. 'I've never tried to produce fashion prints like I've seen in magazines.'

'Exactly!' Claudia lent forward, enthusiasm in her voice. 'I don't want those kind of pictures, I'm not making those kind of clothes.' She tugged apologetically at the finely-embroidered collar of her coat. 'We had to dress so formally in Paris. Ridiculous things, most of the time so that you could hardly move at all. So many women are taking up more strenuous activities now.

'Those are the clothes I am making, practical clothes for playing sport, riding bicycles, climbing mountains, even. Several of my clients are keen aviators, flying their own aeroplanes. I don't want pictures of women standing there like trussed-up dolls but, active, doing things. Something only a woman photographer could truly understand.'

'Of course!' The enthusiasm was catching, and Menna found herself swept along by it. 'I'd love to.' She stopped, reality hitting hard. 'But I don't have a darkroom,' she added, miserably.

'Oh, I think we can manage that.' It was David Llewelyn, looking up from his sketching. 'It seems to me you'll need to set up your own photographic studio, Claudia, if you are really serious about this. I'd be prepared to fund that — for a good return on my investment, of course,' he added with a grin, 'I'm not supporting the enemy out of the goodness of my heart, you know.'

'We'll leave you to think it over, Miss Williams,' Claudia said. 'We're staying at the Prince's Arms until we find a place of our own to purchase. If you would like to bring your answer there when you are ready, you'll be very welcome.'

'Thank you,' Menna said, as Aunt Margaret came in with the tea. Her thoughts were in a whirl, but foremost amongst them the utter relief that this unexpected proposition seemed to be designed to save her. She'd think about it, but of course her answer would be, 'yes.' She'd be a fool to make it otherwise.

And then she could give in her notice at Bryn Hyfryd at the earliest possible opportunity, and leave the perilous temptations of the Lloyd brothers far behind.

8

Menna walked along Conwy quay in the afternoon light, watching the fishermen bringing in their catch. The sea air cleared her head a little as gulls squawked above, and the last of the day's tourists were being escorted down from the ruin of the castle and into the waiting automobiles that roared them off in a cloud of strong-smelling fumes to their guesthouses and hotels.

How quickly things could change, she mused. This morning she had been all confusion, not sure what to think and where to turn, and now, unexpectedly, her way was clear.

Within months, weeks, even, she could be back here in her home town, living within Conwy's ancient walls, and earning her living at the job she loved. And she would be safe, not even Guto Makepeace would be foolish enough to try anything with an employee of David Llewelyn's daughter.

David Llewelyn was rich and famous, and everyone knew him. Menna had heard his name mentioned several times as she walked around the town. With his new gallery opening up in the next few weeks in the same street as his daughter's business, no-one would be about to risk a quarrel with him.

'I wonder if he still thinks of her,' came the thought slipping into Menna's mind. What had happened on that day of the last flight of the *Dragonfly*? And if he hated Gwenan, why had he returned to live so close? Unless Tal was right, and he might well be looking for means to hurt her.

Menna sighed. She couldn't help it, part of her liked Gwenan Lloyd, despite the chill exterior of her employer. If her plight really was so desperate that she might lose her home, thought Menna, guiltily, she would need all the help she could get. And maybe she could still take the *Dragonfly* on one final voyage, and win the bet that would enable her to stay in her home.

All the same, Menna told herself, it was none of her business. Miss Lloyd would not thank her for an employee's sympathy, and Menna had concerns enough of her own. Deep in contemplation, Menna was no longer watching where she was going, and the hand on her arm seemed to come out of nowhere, pinning her to the spot. 'Ouch,' she exclaimed, indignantly, 'that hurts!'

'Well then you'd better stand still,' came an all-too-familiar voice. 'Didn't you hear me calling you?'

'Tal!' she swung round, fighting to get free of him. 'What are you doing here?' His grip closed even firmer round her arm, and when she looked up at him his eyes were cold.

'And I might ask you what you are doing with David Llewelyn,' he shot back.

'That's my business, and none of

your concern,' she returned.

'Really?'

'Really.'

'I thought you hadn't met him before that day on the beach.'

'I hadn't.'

'So your aunt is in the habit of allowing strange men to visit you, then, is she?'

'I beg your pardon?' Her temper was rising.

'You know what I mean.'

'No I don't. I can guess, of course, knowing the unpleasant way your mind works, but you'll leave my aunt out of this if you please. Now let me go.'

'Or else?' he demanded, with heavy sarcasm.

'Or else, Mr Taliesin, you might find yourself at the bottom of the Conwy trussed up tight in a fishing net.'

'Really?'

'Really.' She looked pointedly to the harbour just below them. He followed her line of gaze to the fishermen on the quay watching them, all thoughts of fish quite gone, and with the nearest of them already in the process of retrieving a heavy oar.

'This is my town, don't forget. My uncle still works the mussel boats when the tourists aren't about. Fishermen are a close-knit community, Mr Lloyd. Take on one, and you take on all of them. And that goes for nieces as well.'

'Ah.' He released her, and stepped back a couple of paces. 'I take your point.'

'You all right, Menna?' the watcher called with the oar.

'Yes, thank you, Gareth. A small matter of business.' She favoured Tal with a glare. 'Just a misunderstanding, that's all.'

'Well if you're sure, like,' Gareth replied, a little unwilling to leave it at that.

'I'll let you know if it isn't,' she returned, giving Tal the sweetest of smiles that did not hide the sharp glint of her teeth for a moment. 'We're just going to sort it out now.' She folded her arms. 'So, Mr Lloyd, you were saying?'

'You know what I was saying, Miss Williams. Llewelyn got you that job with my aunt so you could do his spying for him. And his dirty work, I shouldn't wonder.'

Menna gazed at him open-mouthed at such injustice. 'Were you born with such a nasty suspicious mind, or did you have to work at it?' she demanded. 'First your brother, now Mr Llewelyn; hasn't it ever occurred to you that I might have got the post of housekeeper because I am good at the work, and your aunt, unlike you, has the brains to spot it?' For a moment she was convinced he was about to burst a blood vessel, but then a certain speculation came into his look.

'So you didn't know David Llewelyn?'

'No, of course I didn't. When was the last time you think I was in Paris?'

'Ah, but you knew he was in Paris.' His tone was unmistakably triumphant.

'Yes. His daughter told me.'

114

'His what?'

'Daughter. She was with him. And very beautiful and elegant she is, too. I dread to think what you might have made of her.'

'Oh.' Tal was starting to look uncomfortable. 'I didn't see her. I just saw Llewelyn going into your aunt's house. Given his history with Gwenan, what was I supposed to think?'

'Well if you ask me, thinking at all is quite beyond you.'

'Menna, you are impossible. Is there ever a moment when you don't speak your mind?'

'Is that supposed to pass as an apology?' she countered. He cleared his throat. 'Well?'

'You are enjoying this, aren't you?'

'You're the one that started it.'

'All right. I give up. I apologise. I'm sorry. I'd go down on my knees if your friends by the boats there were not still looking so eager for blood.'

'The apology will do,' she returned, swallowing a smile.

There was a moment's silence. Menna became acutely aware that the fishermen might have resumed their work, but to a man they had been following this exchange closely.

There was no way, after that little sparring match, that any of them was about to believe this was a simple matter of business. By the look on Tal's face the same thought was dawning on Tal. He cleared his throat, awkwardly.

'I hope you had a pleasant afternoon, Miss Williams,' he resumed, with exaggerated formality, rather louder than was necessary.

'Yes, thank you, Mr Lloyd,' Menna replied, also loud enough for the men on the quay to hear quite clearly. 'I was speaking with David Llewelyn and his daughter. They are settling in Conwy, you know.'

'Are they now.' He was still managing to be polite, but he couldn't quite hide the grinding of his teeth at this information.

'Miss Llewelyn came to offer me a job.'

'A job?' That jolted him. His eyes narrowed, as if suspecting her of deliberately provoking him. 'Are you serious?'

'Of course. I'm well-known on my own behalf, for my skills as a photographer. You needn't look so surprised that a successful business woman might wish to employ me.' She saw him frown.

'As what?'

'A photographer, naturally. Working as part of her business, with my own studio and darkroom, taking publicity photographs of women's sportswear.' There was a moment's silence.

'So you'll be leaving us,' Tal said, at last.

'Maybe. I haven't decided yet. I have until next week to make my answer.'

'Of course you'll say yes. How could you not say yes to such an offer?'

There was a brief struggle in his face, then he grasped her hands, braving the sudden close attention this attracted from the unloading fishermen. 'You'd be a fool to turn it down, Menna. It's what you want to do. Even if fashion photography isn't what you wish to do all your life it's the chance to make a reputation for yourself. This will be the making of you.'

'I know,' she replied. She should be relieved that he was prepared to let her go so easily, but instead she felt overcome with a terrible emptiness she didn't care to explain to herself. 'I wouldn't start for a month or so. They're still setting things up here. I can still finish your photographs. Maybe I could take further commissions from you if they work out,' she suggested, hesitantly.

'Maybe,' he replied.

'I'm sorry about the darkroom, and the equipment you bought.'

'Oh that,' he gave a rueful smile. 'That's what I was on my way to tell you. Most of the big things on your list weren't in stock, I had to order them. I was cursing all the way back, but I suppose that is my good fortune now, it

118

will save me no end of money.'

'But what about the photographs?'

'Oh, we're still going to do them. It's more urgent than ever, now. My aunt has had an offer for Bryn Hyfryd.'

'An offer? But I didn't know it was for sale.'

'It isn't. At least, it wasn't. But it's no secret on the island the state Gwenan's finances are in. Someone must have decided to jump the gun and get in there before it is put on the open market.'

'Who?'

'No idea. It's through a London solicitor. Could be anyone. It's a low offer, even for the house as it is. The trouble is, she may not get a better, or even one at all. There aren't many people round here with enough wealth to do all the work it would take to bring it up to being a half decent home in most people's eyes. Modernising the plumbing alone would cost a fortune. I'm counting on those photographs to bring in the tourists, or even start

Gwenan seriously thinking about fulfilling that bet.'

'But we haven't got a darkroom.'

'Oh yes we have. At least, you have. Right here in Conwy.'

'Tal, no . . . '

'Why not? You're still a partner. That darkroom in *Makepeace & Williams* is still half yours.'

'*Williams & Makepeace*,' she corrected, absently.

'That's the spirit. I'm sure Makepeace will listen to sense, and a handsome payment for its use.'

'Tal, I can't.'

'Why not?'

'I'm not going back in there — ' she stopped herself just in time, but he had already read her mind.

' — on your own,' he supplied. She nodded, miserably. Out of the corner of her eye she saw his jaw tighten. 'I suppose you wouldn't care to enlighten me as to what exactly young Makepeace tried the last time you were there?' he enquired, evenly.

'No.'

'So I take it it's the sort of thing he'd try again? Nothing personal, just the kind of favour he'd show to any lone female out of earshot of assistance.'

'Yes,' she muttered.

'Well that settles it, then. You'll need a bodyguard. And don't you look like that, young lady. I was known as a fair boxer when I was at school, and while I may not be a crack shot I've been around firearms just enough to look convincing.'

'This isn't a joking matter,' she retorted, fighting a temptation to burst into laughter at the vision this information conjured.

'Who's joking?' he returned, with a grin. 'Or don't you trust me?'

'Of course I trust you.'

'Ah. So maybe you don't trust yourself? Alone in a darkroom with the man of your dreams . . .'

'Don't flatter yourself,' she shot back, aware that her flaming cheeks were rather spoiling the effect. 'It's only your money I'm after.'

'Ouch. Now that is plain speaking indeed. Very well, then. If you promise to behave yourself — '

'Me behave myself?' she exclaimed, indignantly.

' — then I'll promise to behave myself, however much the temptation, and be the perfect bodyguard-cum-assistant, and we'll have those prints to take back to Aunt Gwenan first thing tomorrow. So is that a deal?'

'Tal — '

'Well? Is it? Perhaps you'd care to ask your friends, if you are in any doubt.'

Menna had quite forgotten the fishermen on the quay, but she now discovered they had abandoned the pretence of working to a man, and were following this exchange closely, and by the smiles on more than one face she knew she had just lost this argument.

'I rather think they're expecting me to kiss you,' Tal added, quietly, his face approaching just a little closer to hers.

Even Gareth seemed to have forgotten his oar and was grinning indulgently. Tal drew a little closer, as if he was quite prepared to fulfil their expectations there and then.

'Don't you dare!' Menna stepped back, her voice, she noted irritably, had a definite shake to it. Which was nothing to the state of her knees at this moment. Thankfully Tal took pity on her.

'Very well, madam. But in the absence of a white charger perhaps you'd care to — ' he held out one arm.

'You're ridiculous, Tal,' she replied, finding she had no other choice but to take it. She half expected the men below them to break into a cheer.

'So now for your aunt and uncle.'

Menna had entirely forgotten the small matter of Aunt Margaret and Uncle Rhys. What on earth would they say to her proposed manner of spending the evening? She gave a quick glance towards her companion. He'd find a way of charming them until kingdom come, she suddenly had no doubt of that at all.

Taliesin Lloyd could no doubt charm anyone into doing anything he pleased. With an air of resignation, she allowed herself to be guided towards her uncle's house.

9

'Urgh! That is vile!' Menna stepped inside the door under the sign *Make-peace & Williams* and gasped as the acrid stench of stale chemical solution caught at the back of her throat.

'That's even worse than when I came in here to see them,' Tal remarked, grimacing. 'No wonder the business is not doing well.' He turned up the gas light, and they moved into the shop.

Menna could have cried. Inside the familiar rooms, nothing was as she remembered it. Dad had always ensured the place was kept scrupulously clean, and the reception area had comfortable seats and fresh flowers.

Now, after just a few short months, it looked down-at-heel, and neglected. The reception area was dingy, while the studio itself was noticeably filthy, with the backdrop of a painted woodland for the clients to pose and look as if they were in some country idyl, torn, and disreputable looking. Menna walked through in silence, until she came to the darkroom itself.

'I should never have left,' she said, in despair, looking around at the half-empty trays of dark yellow solution, and the mass of discarded prints on the floor. Every surface was damp and stained with the remainder of chemicals that filled the air with their harsh vapours.

'Sounds to me like you had no choice,' Tal said, looking round in disgust.

'I can't work in this. Dad would never have let things get this bad, some of those developing chemicals can make you really ill, he was always so insistent on spills being mopped up straight away. Besides, it spoils the prints with marks. It will take hours to clean.'

'Don't worry, Menna. We'll have this ship-shape in no time. You just tell me what goes where, and which bits are likely to kill me, and we'll have it good as new.'

Menna smiled at him, glad he was with her to face this disaster. It had been worth it just to see Sam Makepeace bluster when they first turned up on his doorstep with their request, and then to practically grovel at the roll of bank notes emerging from Tal's pocket.

It had been worth it even more when they came across Guto lurking in the corridor, listening to everything that went on in the parlour and clearly hoping to have a share in the good fortune himself.

The expression on Tal's face had left Guto in no doubt that the well-dressed gentleman with Menna knew exactly what had taken place that night at the studio, and was quite prepared to mete out summary justice there and then. The look on Guto's narrow features had been a sight Menna would keep with her for years.

Between them it took less time than

Menna had expected. Fortified by a couple of steaming hot pies from the baker's down the road, and a message sent with the boy from next door explaining the reasons for the delay to Aunt Margaret, they then set about the serious business of the evening.

Menna printed the first picture on to a sheet of paper, and then dipped the invisible image into a tray of fresh solution. Slowly the shape of Conway Castle, and the town within the walls began to emerge in various tones of black and white.

'That's it! That's wonderful, Menna.'

'You can't be sure yet, not in this light,' she warned, placing the picture in the tray of fixing solution. 'Once it's washed we can have a look.' Washing seemed to take ages, but at last she held the finished print in her hands. 'All right, you can turn on the light now,' she said.

They both stared at the gleaming wet print glistening in Menna's hands, blinking in the sudden brightness of light.

'Oh my goodness,' Tal breathed. 'That is so beautiful. You can even see the grass growing in the castle walls.'

'It's not bad,' she admitted.

'Not bad? Not bad? What kind of a perfectionist are you?'

'A perfect one,' she replied with a smile, not quite able to hide her satisfaction. 'It's better than I feared it might be.'

'No-one will be able to resist that, Menna. We'll have tourists flocking in their millions. And as for Gwenan . . . ' He was smiling. 'Just one look and I'd bet my aeroplane she'll be itching to get back up in the *Dragonfly*.'

'I hope so.' Menna sighed, hanging up the print to dry on a line above their heads. 'Ready for the next one?'

'Ready.'

★   ★   ★

The print of Conwy was definitely the best of the ones they printed that night. Several showed the shake Menna had feared, but most had Tal exclaiming in delight. The view of Snowdon was as clear as could be, with the train clearly visible, while many of the other mountain ranges were even more dramatic in their varying shades of grey than Menna remembered them.

'I call that an unqualified success,' Tal said, as they left late in the evening, the precious sheaf of prints tucked safely beneath his arm.

'I'd like to try some of them again,' Menna said, frowning in concentration at the improvements she would like to make.

'Of course. We can do this for as long as it takes. But these show what can be done, even on a first attempt. They'll be enough to show Gwenan what we mean, and at least put off that offer until we have given this a chance.' His voice was full of energy and enthusiasm, as if he had suddenly been given a new lease of life.

'I'm glad they worked out well,' Menna said. They were walking along the harbour, beneath the castle wall. The sea was calm, and a half moon glided in between whisping trails of cloud. Tomorrow she would be back at Bryn Hyfryd, and back to reality. But tonight, walking through the quiet night with her arm tucked companionably inside Tal's, Menna felt she had never been so happy in all her life.

'I'd better go,' she said, at last, regretfully, seeing the light in the kitchen of the fisherman's cottage tucked under the wall. 'Aunt Margaret is waiting for me.'

'Just so long as it isn't your uncle with a shotgun,' Tal remarked, with a smile.

'Don't be daft. He gave me the shotgun to hide beneath my coat,' she returned. 'You don't think he'd trust a gentleman, do you?' She felt Tal chuckle. 'You think I'm not serious?'

'Well I might, if I hadn't been eyeing that very neat form of yours so closely for the past hours, and I saw plenty that was very pleasing, but nothing approaching a shotgun.'

'Tal!' she was glad the night was dark to hide the colour in her cheeks. 'You were supposed to be working. And behaving.'

'Well I couldn't help having a quick peek, every now and then, could I? I'm only human.'

'Tal Lloyd, you are incorrigible. What am I going to do with you?'

'Marry me?' came back the unexpected reply. There was a moment's silence.

'What did you say?'

'Marry me.'

'Don't be ridiculous.'

'I'm serious, Menna. I've never been so serious in my life.'

'I can't marry you!'

'Why not?'

'Your aunt wouldn't approve.'

'I'm not marrying to please my aunt, especially if it takes a ninny like Charlotte Wynn to do the trick, and I have a brave, beautiful, fiery little imp like you standing so close to me.'

'I — ' The sudden intensity in his voice had that treacherous heart of hers pounding away again. He couldn't mean it. Men like him didn't marry girls like her.

It was the heat of the moment, the deceptive closeness born of working so hard together on a project that both of them were so passionate about.

She was a sensible girl, she'd never fallen for this kind of thing before. All she needed was to be sensible now, and send him packing with a flea in his ear and no doubts that she wasn't one to be won over so lightly. Instead, Menna found herself floundering.

'Well, well, Miss Williams,' he said softly, his lips dangerously close to her ear, 'that's not at all like you to come up with no real reason at all.'

'I'll think of something,' she returned, grimly.

'Perhaps I should point out that the most obvious one is that you don't love me,' he remarked lightly.

'I — ' Much to her humiliation, the

floundering was getting worse, and the lie just would not come. Not love him? It came to her in an overwhelming rush just how much she loved him. How much she would always love him, however impossible that love might be, she reflected, sadly. She was a fool to even let the treacherous dream creep anywhere near her heart.

'Aha! You just can't say it.' It was the triumph in his voice, and the creeping of his arms about her, and his face drawing closer to hers that stung Menna into action.

'Go away!' she exclaimed, bringing her foot smartly down on his.

'Menna! I wasn't going to — '

'Oh yes you were.' She was unimpressed by his tone of injured innocence. 'D'you really think it'll take one kiss and I'll be all yours?' Well, all right, it would, but there was no need to give him the advantage of letting him know this.

'Menna,' he breathed, still close enough to send shivers down her spine.

but Menna had come to her senses, and inspiration had struck, and she wasn't about to give in now.

'I'm still employed by your aunt, and you know what she feels about house-keepers setting their caps at her nephews.' That worked. She was ashamed at the complete lack of relief in her body as he stepped back. He gazed at her thought-fully.

'I can wait.'

'Tal, I'm just about to start a new post. The kind of work I've always wanted to do, all my life. I can't give that up now, I might never get another chance again.'

'Who said I didn't want a working wife?' All of a sudden he was laughing again, edging himself closer, while keeping out of range of her boots that were looking dangerous once more. 'They're not unknown, you know. This is the twentieth century, after all, and if you women are aiming to get the vote you'll have to be prepared to work for it. Besides, as Gwenan says, I've got expensive tastes to keep up.'

'Tal!' she exclaimed indignantly, caught off guard, her laughter threatening to undo her dignified pose all together.

'There you are, you see. You can't resist me.'

'I suppose you say that to all the girls,' she snapped back, instantly.

'No, Menna, I don't. I don't exactly send them to line up at my door. I never planned this, but you're the best thing that ever came into my life, and I don't want to lose you.'

He took her hands gently in his, his voice serious once more. 'I'll leave you alone, Menna. I promise I won't mention this again while you are still working for my aunt. I don't want to put you in an impossible position. But once you are working for Miss Llewelyn you will be free of Gwenan and Bryn Hyfryd, and be an independent business woman. There will be nothing then to stop me calling on you. And if you tell me not to, I'll never bother you again.

But I hope you will let me, Menna, with all my heart, so that we can start again.'

Under cover of darkness, Menna smiled. When he was like this, he was totally irresistible. She took a deep breath.

'I would like that,' she said, warily, not quite sure where such an admittance might lead.

'Good.' He gave her hands a quick squeeze, and then, as good as his word, released them.' Now you'd better get inside.

* * *

It was just after dawn the next day, that the little aeroplane banked over the grounds of Bryn Hyfryd, and taxied to a halt in front of the shed by the sea front.

'You'd better go in,' Tal said, helping Menna slide down to the ground. 'I'll tell Gwenan I had engine trouble on the way back from Chester and had to stay n Conwy overnight. That should be an

137

innocent enough reason for giving you a lift back.'

'I hope so.' Menna smiled.

'Just so long as I look as if I view you as the ground beneath my feet, we should be safe enough,' he remarked, gloomily.

'Tal — ' Menna was not listening, his head turned sharply at the unaccustomed edge of anxiety in her voice.

'What is it?'

'The doors to the shed, they're not properly closed. They were locked last night. I checked.'

'Damn thieves! I've had trouble with them before.' Sure enough, the huge doors that let the aeroplane in and out were swinging slowly to and fro in the breeze. 'The lock's been forced,' Tal said, inspecting them. 'Looks like a professional job to me. Well, at least the 'plane wasn't inside,' he added, philosophically, peering around the inside of the shed. 'They must have been disappointed. Doesn't look as if much is missing.'

He opened the doors fully, allowing

as much light in as possible as he prowled round the building. Menna followed him. Nothing seemed to be disturbed, not even the small tools hung up on the walls that could easily have been stashed into a pocket. It was all very strange. 'Ah, well,' Tal was saying, 'I'll just have to mend this lock and have one of the men guard the place until we can put in better security. We can't afford to lose the 'plane now.'

As they made their way out Menna's eyes fell on the row of fuel cans next to the door. Instantly she knew something was wrong. One of them was missing. She could see the small puddle of fuel left where one of them had been moved, leaving a gap in the next row. Fuel was expensive. Each can cost more money than she could ever dream of seeing.

She paused, staring down at them. But why only take one? The cans were heavy to carry, making it impossible to escape quickly. Why take all the risk of breaking into the place and struggling off with just one? If the thieves had hoped to steal an entire aeroplane, or even some of its parts, they must have had transport. In which case they would surely not have left much that was valuable behind . . .

Cold suddenly gripped at Menna's heart. She whirled around, her eyes knowing exactly what they would see as she peered into the darkness at the back of the shed.

Sure enough, the door to the inner room was slightly open. Tal must have missed it in his intent scrutiny of the shelves and walls of the main part of the building. She grabbed his arm.

'The *Dragonfly*,' she whispered.

'What?'

She was close behind him as he strode over to the little door and pushed it open fully. Inside there remained only a few tattered shreds of silk to show that the *Dragonfly* had ever been there.

10

'It must have happened last night. Those doors were locked, I'm sure of it,' Menna said, her heart crying out at the despair on Tal's face. 'They can't have gone far, not with such a big thing as the *Dragonfly*.'

'I don't think stealing her was the point,' Tal replied, tightly. 'I expect she's in a thousand pieces by now.'

'But we can at least have a look. It's worth a try.' She was all ready to set off there and then, but Tal was bending down, running his hands along the planks of the floorboards. 'Ah, here it is,' he exclaimed, prising one of the boards up, and lifting out a small tin.

'The *Dragonfly* was Gwenan's own design,' he explained. 'At least her plans are still here.' He pressed the tin into Menna's hands. 'You take them Menna. Hide them, take them with you when you next go to your uncle's and find a safe place where no-one would think of looking.'

'But no-one would know there were still plans in existence,' Menna protested.

'Oh, I can think of someone who would,' he replied, grimly, making his way outside.

★ ★ ★

It seemed to Menna that they searched for hours, up and down the coastline either side of the shed for any trace of the missing *Dragonfly*, but with not a trace to be found.

'Over here!' she heard Tal call at last. She ran over to join him at the edge of the next large sweep of bay. There in front of them on the grass lay the smoking remains of a fire, with blackened and shrivelled pieces of silk scattered around its edges by the wind.

'So that's it then,' he remarked, flatly. 'Burning her is pretty final.'

'I can't see the basket, though,' Menna said, poking at the ashes with a long stick. 'There aren't any bits of it here at all. It wouldn't have burned away completely, and anyhow, wouldn't it have made too much smoke and attracted attention?'

'Well, he can't have dragged it much farther than this. It's far too heavy.'

Menna frowned, pondering his words. As she did so her eyes rested on the beach below her.

'The tide,' she said at last. 'Tal — '

'Yes?'

'If the balloon came down in the ocean, would the basket float?'

'Yes, that's what it was designed to do.'

'I thought so.' She stood there, her eyes carefully scanning the waves.

'What is it, Menna?'

'The tide's going out. From the marks on the rocks it must be quite deep here at high tide.'

'Deep enough to push the basket over and be sure it would float! Of course.' His eyes followed hers. 'And once it gets out into that tidal stream, it'll be out to sea in no time. No need to take the time to destroy it, the waves will do that surely enough.'

'There!' Menna's eyes could just make out the dark shape bobbing on the water, perilously far out.

'Damn,' he cursed, feelingly, 'It'll be out of the bay in minutes, and then we'll lose it.' Before Menna could realise what he was about, he had thrown off his jacket and shoes and was scrambling down the beach into the water.

Tal was a strong swimmer, and helped by the outgoing tide, he reached the basket in minutes. He swam around to the far side, and was soon struggling to push it back towards the shore in front of him. But the basket was big and heavy, and this time the tide was working against him. Menna could see the outward pull of the water overpowering his efforts and pushing both him and the basket out towards the wide strip of tidal current snaking out into the merciless expanse of the Irish Sea.

Once sucked into the current, not even the strongest of swimmers would ever be able to make their way back. He would be swept out to sea, until he was exhausted by the cold and the effort of keeping afloat, and would surely drown.

'Tal!' It took Menna only a moment to strip away her hampering skirts, and down to her underwear, and to rush headlong after him.

The water was cold. Bitterly cold. She gasped as the first wave swept over her, numbing her from head to foot. But Menna had lived near water all her life. Menna struck out strongly, the action sending the blood flowing through her veins, keeping the freezing waters at bay. Within minutes she had reached him.

'You're a fool,' he muttered, breathlessly, as she took the other side of the basket.

She took a quick glance over her shoulder. Tal had managed to hold his own, but the tidal race seemed ever closer, lapping at the smooth surface o the sea with an ominous power. 'If we get caught up in that we'll have n chance,' she said. 'If we get too clos we'll just have to let the basket go.'

'Over my dead body,' Tal muttered with a grim humour, pushing hi shoulder firmly against his end of th basket. The closeness of disaster gav them both a strength they never knew they had.

Menna felt the basket move, and then slowly begin to inch itself agains the flow of the tide towards the shore By the time she dared look back again the current was a dark line, safely in th distance, and her searching feet foun the anchor of the sandy floor.

Between them, they hauled th battered remains of the *Dragonfly* on t the beach, and collapsed into a exhausted heap beside her.

'Very fetching,' Tal remarked, rollin over on to his stomach to watch a Menna attempted to brush the san from her bodice and bloomers. She looked up with a smile and a faint blush. 'You should suggest to Miss Llewelyn that she creates a line of women's sports clothes to that design.' He grinned.

'Idiot,' she replied. 'Claudia says some women use men's trousers for cycling already.'

'Long may it last,' he said, with another grin. He hauled himself up, and became serious again. 'You'd better get back to the house, Menna. They'll have seen the aeroplane land, and Gwenan will get suspicious enough at the two of us coming back together without there being a gap between our landing and arrival. I'd better hide this as best I can.' His lips brushed hers lightly, with a touch of salt, and sand. 'Thank you, Menna. I could never have done this without you.'

'Are you sure the *Dragonfly* will be all right?'

'Oh yes,' he replied. 'I'll make sure of that. Aunt Gwenan has to believe me this time. Surely she can't be so blind. And if she is, there's nothing I can do, and I shall just have to whisk you away to the mainland and start my flying ambitions elsewhere.'

Menna climbed up the bank up to the cliff edge and pulled on her skirt and top over her damp underclothes, and fastened her boots. Then, grabbing her camera case and smoothing her hair down as much as possible, she made her way as fast as she could towards Bryn Hyfryd.

★　★　★

She should have known, the moment she walked through the door. The house was quiet, ominously quiet. The thought struck her, and then was pushed away.

'Miss Williams!' Gwenan Lloyd's voice from the library could have matched an iceberg.

'Yes, Miss Lloyd?' Menna paused on the first stair, a sense of foreboding churning in her stomach.

'I would be grateful if you could favour me with an interview.' Even more ominous. Menna took a deep breath, and made her way into the library.

'Good morning, Miss Lloyd.' Feeling very nervous, and slightly foolish, Menna stood before her employer, and tried not to drip seawater on to the thick pile of the carpet.

'What do you mean, returning to my house like this?'

'I — er — ' Fell in the water? Decided to go for a morning swim? One look at those grey eyes, and Menna knew it was the truth, or nothing. 'I'm sorry, Miss Lloyd, I — ' Menna stopped. There, just behind his aunt, leaning nonchalantly against the bookcase with just the faintest of smirks on his face, was Rhodri.

'Yes, Miss Williams?'

Menna's mind worked fast. What was it Tal had said? He knew someone who would know about the plans for the

149

Dragonfly. He. Tal had referred to the thief as 'he'.

It was the smirk that convinced her. The charm had gone, as if he had achieved his aim and no longer needed it, leaving a cruel twist to his lips at the sight of her discomfiture, and a hard gleam to his eyes.

Rhodri. Who else could it be? Rhodri with the expensive tastes, and a certain Lady Charlotte to impress. Rhodri who could easily have seen that she had checked the shed each night while Tal was away, and knew they were both away last night.

Rhodri who would have known about Gwenan's bet, and the significance of the *Dragonfly*, and who had as much as anyone to gain from its destruction, and must never find out that he had failed and what Tal was up to at this very moment. Not if they were to have any hope of saving the *Dragonfly*. Menna swallowed.

'I'm sorry, Miss Lloyd. I can't tell you.'

'You can't tell me?' Gwenan's pale face flushed in indignation. 'What kind of answer is that to make?' Her eyes glanced towards Rhodri. 'I take it this has a lot do with my elder nephew.'

'This has noting to do with Tal — I mean Mr Lloyd,' Menna said quickly. She bit her lip at the slip and winced, waiting for the next onslaught. Tried and sentenced out of her own mouth, it seemed, given the triumph in Rhodri's eye. But at least it was keeping his mind away from the whereabouts of his brother.

'I see.' Well, that tone smacked of the hung, drawing and quartering, if ever anything did. Menna swallowed. 'And you've nothing else to say on the matter, Miss Williams?'

'No, Miss Lloyd. I'm sorry.'

'And I'm sorry I was mistaken in you. You will go up to your room now and make yourself presentable. When you come down again, you can collect your wages, and I expect you to leave the house that instant.'

'Yes, Miss Lloyd.' If she drew this out long enough, maybe Tal would be back, and ready to explain, but the words sent a chill through her heart and any such consideration out of her head.

'I'll take Miss Williams to the station, Aunt. We owe her that much.'

'Thank you, Rhodri,' Gwenan held out her hand to him and smiled affectionately. 'After what you have told me, it's more than I could have expected you to do.' She turned back to Menna whose very blood had frozen as if she were still struggling in the waves far from the shore. 'I hope you will be grateful, young lady. It's more than you deserve after your behaviour.'

'Very,' Menna murmured, eyes firmly on the floor. Heaven knows what antics she was supposed to have got up to, but whatever they were, Miss Lloyd was not about to take any argument. Whatever he had told his aunt, Menna could see in the cold glint in his eyes that Rhodri at least guessed that Tal had told her about the *Dragonfly*.

At the very least she was a witness, someone who would confirm Tal's story. Once in that automobile, Menna had a distinct impression that wherever she might end up, it would most certainly not be at the railway station.

She forced herself to smile, and her eyes to look up empty of any thought. 'Thank you, Mr Rhodri. That is kind of you. I shall just collect my belongings. I shall be as quick as I can.' And with a quick bob of a curtsey, she was out of the room, and making her way up the stairs, trying to sound as unhurried in her movements as possible.

Menna paused on the second floor landing. Once she got to her room in the attic, she knew there would be no way out. She had to keep calm and find an escape route. Below, she could hear Miss Lloyd, still in the library, clearly upset, and Rhodri's voice soothing her.

No-one was following her to see if she was about to make off with the family silver, and thanks to her calm exterior, Rhodri seemed to have no suspicion that she had any idea of trying to escape. Maybe he thought she believed he really would simply take her to the station, satisfied that no-one would ever believe her.

If she was to stand a chance at all, she had to make her escape now. The library was at the front of the house. If she was to get out without being seen or heard, her only way was through the back of Bryn Hyfryd.

Thank heaven her job meant she knew each room like the back of her hand! There was no sign of Tal returning, and by the time he did, it could well be too late. There was only one chance for her, and Menna had to take it.

Miss Lloyd's bedroom was next to hers, situated at the back of the house. Slipping off her boots, and walking as gingerly as possible, avoiding the loose floorboards that would have creaked and betrayed her, Menna made her way across to Miss Lloyd's window.

She tied her laces so her boots sa

round her neck, swung herself out, and down with the help of the drainpipe on to the roof of the kitchen below her. Moving quickly now, she wriggled her way along to where stout trellising held the faded remains of last year's wisteria blossoms.

Menna landed on the gravel of the drive without incident, and adjusted the position of her camera box swung across her back. All was calm. In the far distance she could hear the roar of an engine as Rhodri started up the automobile to bring it round to the front of the house.

With one last glance around her, Menna made a run for the woods at the edge of the kitchen garden, her boots clutched firmly in one hand.

11

She was cold, and she was wet, and she was more terrified than she had ever been in her life before. Menna looked up towards the sky. The rain had begun again, but the cloud above her raced in the wind that had blown up as darkness fell, revealing the tiny sliver of moon once again.

There were no stars to be seen, but as a fishermen's niece, Menna had learnt to judge direction by every means at her disposal. The faint glow gave her just enough to guess her right path.

All that day she had aimed across the fields and the moorland towards the distant mountains on the mainland, and the safety of the Menai Straights. If she could only reach Beaumaris she was confident she could persuade the fishermen to take her out to find a boat willing to take her back to Conwy maybe even to Uncle Rhys himself if he was braving the waves that night.

The fishing community was small enough for word to have got around that Rhys Williams' niece was working up at the big house. Whatever Rhodri might tell them, that would be enough to get her a safe passage across. Or so she hoped.

Rhodri had plenty of money at his disposal, and she was quite sure he would be prepared to offer a large bribe for her return . . . But best not to think of that eventuality.

During the first hours of her escape, she had heard the engines of an aeroplane circling overhead, distant, but coming nearer, as if Tal guessed which way she might be heading. At first that had given her hope, but then the louder roar of another engine had begun to encircle her, too.

More than once the roar had sounded uncomfortably near, forcing her to cower in the nearest ditch, or wait for what seemed hours in the nearest clump of trees, until she heard it make its way into the distance again.

She had not dared show herself long enough to attract the attention of the aeroplane. Besides, if Rhodri saw the machine circling over one place he would know where to look . . . Maybe Tal had had the same idea, or maybe it was the deteriorating weather conditions, but as darkness had begun to creep across the endless expanse of fields there was no longer the sound of the 'plane, just the roar of the automobile, and the streak of headlights appearing all around her.

It was back again. As the roar stopped at the entrance to the pathway, Menna froze, and then grasped the branch of the oak tree above her head, pulling herself into its branches with a squelch of sodden boots. In the harsh light of the headlamps she could just make out the figure of Rhodri making his way slowly down the little path.

He must have guessed these were the routes she was taking, she realised with an inward shudder. If he guessed where she was heading, all he had to do was to get ahead of her, stop the engine, and wait in the darkness for her to reach him . . .

'Damn!' His curse spat out at her from below her place of refuge. 'Useless cattle!' One glance upwards and he would see her, but Rhodri was too preoccupied with scrapping the leavings of a passing cow off his shoes on the wet grass at the side of the trackway. At least that appeared to distract him, the next moment he was striding back to the comfort of the automobile.

As she was about to lower herself back on to the track, Menna paused. A familiar smell had been propelled on the wind towards her. The smell of Salt, and of fish and seaweed. She was nearer the sea than she had thought.

Menna left the track, and struck off through the trees, following the distant sound of waves breaking on the shore.

★　★　★

'Are you sure this is a good idea?' David Llewelyn looked up from his sketch pad to where his daughter was running long seams of silk through her Singer sewing machine.

'Of course, Papa. Those plans were quite clear.'

'Gwenan still might not want anything to do with the *Dragonfly* at all.'

'We'll see,' Claudia said with a smile. 'But at least this proves that we are on her side.'

'I'm hoping Tal can persuade her of that,' David returned, with an air of gloom. 'She can be stubborn as can be. Fancy allowing that poor girl . . . '

'Shh,' Claudia said, glancing over to the figure curled up in a chair by the window.

'It's all right, I'm not asleep,' Menna said, opening her eyes, a little unwillingly.

'Don't get up.' Claudia was on her feet in a moment. 'I'll make a cup of tea. I'm sure you can do with one, Menna.'

'Did you see Tal, Mr Llewelyn?' Menna turned in her chair, anxiously.

'Yes, I did Menna. And frantic with worry he was at you disappearing like that. He was blaming himself for all kinds of things.'

'He wasn't to know what Rhodri was planning, or that he had Miss Lloyd ready for when I came back,' Menna said, gently.

'I know, but that still didn't stop him. At least it made him more determined than ever to try and make Gwenan listen to him.' He smiled at her. 'And you should have seen the expression on his face when I told him you were safe, and staying with me and Claudia until all this blows over.'

'Oh,' Menna said, feeling herself blush.

'And I never thought I'd see the day,' David added, dryly. 'A Lloyd boy well and truly tamed. You're a remarkable young woman, Menna, as well as a brave one.'

'I don't know about the remarkable,

and I'm certainly not brave,' she returned with a grimace. 'I was terrified all the time on the way back.' She shivered.

She had waited almost until the last moment, until they were putting the boats out to sea, before she had dared emerge from her hiding place beneath the round towers of Beaumaris Castle, and run down to the sea shore, every moment expecting to find herself caught in the merciless shine of Rhodri's headlights, or for the fishermen to throw her into some cabin until he came to fetch her. She never wanted to do anything like that, ever again.

An abrupt knocking had her jumping nervously in her seat. Claudia appeared, a worried expression on her face.

'Papa?'

'Don't worry. There is nothing Rhodri can do to us here.' David quietly took a revolver from the shelf beside him and put it in his pocket. 'I'll answer the door.'

'Don't worry, Menna, it will be all

right,' Claudia said, smiling at her new friend. They heard the door opened, and a rapid exchange.

'You have no right to enter my house . . . ' David's voice was loud, and angry, but to little effect as footsteps made their way rapidly towards them.

'I'll go where I choose. I don't need your permission, thank you.' Menna's eyes widened at the imperious tone of the voice, and the next minute Gwenan Lloyd swept into the room. 'Stay where you are,' commanded the visitor as Menna attempted to stand up. 'You can hear everything I have to say from there, young lady.' She saw Menna's eyes slide instinctively past her. 'Oh, and I suppose you are looking for support back there,' she added, tartly, as David Llewelyn accompanied another figure following her into the room.

'Tal!' Menna saw his tall form duck into the room with relief. 'Mr Lloyd,' she added finding Gwenan's grey eyes fixed upon her. All the same, she didn't care. Not even Miss Lloyd's severity could diminish the expression she had seen in his eyes.

'Would you care to take a seat, Gwenan,' David Llewelyn asked, politely.

'No, I would not.'

'Aunt — ' Tal was clearly in despair at his relative's complete lack of any kind of manners.

'I can say my piece standing up, Taliesin, if you don't mind.' Gwenan Lloyd cleared her throat, and turned to Menna. 'Miss Williams — ' There was a moment's silence as she appeared to have difficulty in finding the words. 'Miss Williams,' she resumed at last. 'I believe I owe you an apology.'

'Oh,' Menna said, to whom this did not sound in the least apologetic at all.

'I believe at our last meeting I passed some unfortunate remark on the subject of your, ah, relations with my nephew. Since they were based on information which I now know to have been, to say the least false . . . '

'It doesn't matter,' Menna put in quickly, seeing the older woman struggle.

'Don't interrupt. And yes it does matter. I've been a fool, and I intend to say so. If I hadn't been, Rhodri would never have got away with — ' she bit her lip, stern voice breaking at last, and fell silent. 'Perhaps I will sit down after all,' she muttered, sinking down into the chair Claudia had been using. 'It's all come as a bit of a shock to me, you see. And he still wouldn't admit it, even after we'd had the accountant through his dealings. He should have come to me if he was in debt, not try to get the home from beneath my feet. And as for making sure I could never fulfil that foolish bet — '

Her eyes, in avoiding all those around her, had landed on the voluminous silk on the table next to her. Humiliation vanishing instantly, her voice was sharp once more. 'What is this?'

'The *Dragonfly*, Gwenan,' David said, gently. 'Tal had given Menna the plans for safekeeping. My daughter is sewing up a new balloon.'

'A new one.' Gwenan looked at the

silk, and there was no disguising the hunger on her face.

'And the basket is quite safe,' Tal put in. 'With all that chasing about the countryside after Menna, Rhodri never did find it.'

'Why don't you fly her, Gwenan?' David said. 'One last time. You can do it easily, and then Bryn Hyfryd will be safe.'

'I can't.'

'Of course you can.'

'No. No David, I can't. Not any more.'

'But — '

'Leave her, Llewelyn,' Tal said, gruffly. 'It's not something anyone should be forced to do. Menna and I have been working on something. There is another way.'

'Very well. But I just want an answer. Why not, Gwenan?'

'It is nothing to do with you,' she retorted.

'Isn't it?' he persisted, gently. 'This last few years, since Claudia's mother died, I've been thinking again over that time. We can all be idiots when we're young, and I rather think I was the prize fool of them all. I thought you meant it when you said you didn't love me, and you never wanted to see me again. My pride was hurt. It never occurred to me it might not be true.'

'It was true. It is true. I'm better off without you. Everything was all right until — ' She stopped, eyeing him, eyes full of pain.

'Until I was a clumsy oaf and got my foot caught in that stupid rope.'

'Yes.' Brittle surface crumbling, she hid her head in her hands. She sat there for a long while without moving. 'You made me afraid,' she said, at last, lifting her face. 'You made me afraid. I'd never felt fear before, however high I'd gone, whatever storms I'd come across. I was never afraid. Not until I saw you hurt. And then I knew how easily I could lose you, lose everything. And I couldn't bear it.

'I was too much of a coward to go up

in the *Dragonfly* again. And I couldn't bear the thought of loving you and losing you,' She gave a bitter laugh. 'Well, I've had my punishment, I've lost the *Dragonfly*, and I lost you, anyhow. And now I'm about to lose my home.'

'Nonsense.' David was looking down at her severely, but with a glow in his eyes Menna had not seen before. 'I'm petrified each time I pick up my brush that I'll fail, but I still go ahead and do it.'

'That's not your life!'

'Love isn't necessarily your life, either,' he retorted. 'All right, I bet Tal still gets nervous each time he takes off.'

'Sick as a dog,' Tal said, feelingly.

Gwenan looked at them both, eyes moving slowly from one to the other, as if a new thought was entering her head.

'So instead of shutting yourself away from the world and building up all the barriers you can lay your hands on, why don't you brave this, just once.'

'On my own,' she murmured doubtfully. 'I'm not sure . . . '

'It doesn't say anything about crew on the ground, in that bet, does it?'

'Well, no . . . '

'Then I can be your crew on the ground. I'll follow you wherever you go, be there when you come down, and be ready to ferry you home if you have had enough. Wherever you go you'll be able to see me.'

'You'd do that? After everything, you'd do that?'

'Of course. And if you dare ask me the question 'why'?, you'd better be prepared for the answer.'

'No thank you, not just now,' she said, hastily, regaining some of her old poise. 'But the house . . . '

'Bryn Hyfryd can survive without you for a few days. You have an excellent housekeeper here in this room. Tal can make sure everything runs smoothly.'

'Hardly a respectable arrangement,' Gwenan said, severely.

'Very well, then. I'm sure Claudia wouldn't mind staying there a few days to act as chaperone.'

'Mmmm.' Gwenan was in deep thought. Menna held her breath. From the look on Tal's face, he was holding his, too. 'No,' said Miss Lloyd at last, loudly and firmly. 'I've got a better idea.'

She caught the dismay on Menna's face, and her mouth slowly broke into a very wide, and very mischievous smile. 'A far better idea. And if you want me to fly the *Dragonfly* at all, I won't take 'no' for an answer.'

12

In the dawn breeze the huge silken folds of the balloon billowed like some low cloud.

'Isn't she lovely?' Tal said.

'The most beautiful thing I've ever seen,' Menna replied. Around them men were rushing to and fro, burning gas to pump hot air into the almost inflated balloon, shouting orders, and trying to avoid the mass of reporters and photographers ranged on the field outside Bryn Hyfryd.

'That doesn't need any more adjusting, you fools.' Gwenan Lloyd's familiar tones floated across the dark air, sending an entire team of helpers scurrying for cover. 'And I don't want you anywhere near those ropes, David,' he added, even more sharply.

'Yes, my dear.'

'Why don't you make yourself useful

and make sure the automobile starts or something,' she remarked, irritably.

'It's nerves,' Tal said. 'I don't know how he puts up with it.'

'Love, I should imagine,' Claudia replied, standing near him, with a wry smile.

'You don't mind, do you?'

'Good heaven's, no. It's good to see him happy again. Besotted suits Papa, and, besides, it make me feel a little less guilty that I am a busy woman now, with not so much time to spend with him any more.'

'There she goes!' The dark flame of gas was switched off, and the balloon swayed majestically on her moorings.

'To the last flight of the *Dragonfly*,' Gwenan called, and this time there was no mistaking the excitement in her voice. 'Let her go!'

There was a moment's pause, then the balloon cleared its moorings and rose slowly into the lightening sky, and over the sea. A ragged cheer went up followed by a rapid fire of photographers, and the start of an automobil engine next to the house.

'I'd better go,' Claudia said, smiling. 'Your uncle offered me a ride back to Conwy. I've never been on a paddle-steamer before, it will be quite an experience. I'll see you next week, Menna. The new sportswear lines should be ready for you to start photographing by then.'

'So soon?' Tal complained.

'No need for you to feel sorry for yourself, Mr Lloyd,' Menna retorted. 'It's only for a few days a week, I'll be at your beck and call for the rest of the time.'

Everyone, it seemed, was leaving, shouting out their good-byes and good lucks and their promises to see them soon, leaving Tal and Menna to stand on the shore watching as the balloon floated into a speck in the distance, a tiny shadow against the rising sun.

'You don't mind?' Tal asked, slipping his arm around her. 'Not having a honeymoon, I mean.'

'You mean I'm to have no honeymoon

of any kind at all? You disappoint me, Mr Lloyd.'

'You know what I mean. Egypt, the Riviera. The world tour.'

'Oh that. No, not particularly. I expect I can persuade you to do all that later. This is the place I'd most like to be at this moment. Especially with no need for any kind of chaperone at all.'

'Good.' The arms tightened, and his breath was warm on her neck. He paused, and she felt him chuckle. 'By the way, Mrs Lloyd, I thought you were supposed to throw your bouquet for the bridesmaids? I was quite sure Claudia would be the lucky woman, instead you just handed it meekly to Gwenan.'

'She told me to,' Menna replied with a smile. 'Last evening, when she came to accompany me to the church. And I don't think a 'no' was an option. Any more than a midnight wedding just hours before she set off was ever an option.'

'Ah. I should have guessed about that. Trust Aunt Gwenan to steal the limelight, even on her own nephew's wedding day.' Menna smiled.

It had been quite clear in the past few weeks that there would be no changing Gwenan Lloyd however hard anyone might try. The icy coldness had quite gone from her eyes, apart from the moment the police had arrived to announce that Rhodri had been arrested trying to board a ferry at Holyhead, when they had been as frozen as glaciers, but her imperious nature would never be tamed at all. The smile turned into a laugh.

'Anyhow, sweetheart,' she muttered, 'I thought I owed it to her since she ordered you to marry me.'

'Yes, and I like the way you refused me when I was making myself as charming as could be, but once my aunt opened her mouth you caved in immediately.'

'Only so that she could complete her bet and not have to worry about what was going on at the house,' she replied demurely.

'Ha!' he said. 'And I thought you just wanted me for my money.'

'Oh, no,' she returned. 'Actually it was for your aeroplane. I've had so many enquiries about those photographs I took from her I can see I shall be world famous before next summer, and then I shall need a pilot at my beck and call to take me up there when the weather conditions seem promising.'

'Why, you little — ' There was a brief scuffle, accompanied by enough laughter to have the departing guests turning their heads to view the source of amusement, which somehow settled down with Menna finding herself even more closely entwined in his arms than before.

'Look, Tal, she's almost round the headland!'

'So she is.' They were both silent as the distant balloon made it carefully round the cliffs, and out of sight.'

'Do you think she'll make it?' Menna's tone was anxious.

'Of course. You should have learnt b

now, my darling, that what Aunt Gwenan sets out to do, Aunt Gwenan invariably achieves. Who else could have persuaded so many guests, not to mention half the press of the land, to stay up all night after our wedding to watch a dawn ascent?'

'So that really is it, the last flight of the *Dragonfly*.' For a moment she felt almost mournful at the thought, but then she heard her husband begin to laugh.

'Well if it is, then I'm a Duchess. Did you see that look on her face when she first saw it sitting there, good as new? I'd say Aunt Gwenan is about to make ballooning rival aeroplanes in popularity. She'll be on the front of every newspaper, just you see. The last flight of the *Dragonfly*? If you ask me, this is only just the beginning.'

We do hope that you have enjoyed reading this large print book.

Did you know that all of our titles are available for purchase?

We publish a wide range of high quality large print books including:
Romances, Mysteries, Classics General Fiction Non Fiction and Westerns

Special interest titles available in large print are:
The Little Oxford Dictionary Music Book, Song Book Hymn Book, Service Book

Also available from us courtesy of Oxford University Press:
Young Readers' Dictionary (large print edition) Young Readers' Thesaurus (large print edition)

For further information or a free brochure, please contact us at:
**Ulverscroft Large Print Books Ltd., The Green, Bradgate Road, Anstey, Leicester, LE7 7FU, England.
Tel:** (00 44) **0116 236 4325
Fax:** (00 44) **0116 234 0205**